International Men of
Sports

AN ACE IN THE
TIEBREAK

T.A. CHASE and
DEVON RHODES

An Ace in the Tiebreak
ISBN # 978-1-78430-256-6
©Copyright T.A. Chase and Devon Rhodes 2014
Cover Art by Posh Gosh ©Copyright September 2014
Interior text design by Claire Siemaszkiewicz
Totally Bound Publishing

Totally Bound Publishing books by T.A. Chase and Devon Rhodes:

International Men of Sports
A Sticky Wicket in Bollywood
Chasing the King of the Mountains
At First Touch
Blindsided
Burning Up the Ice
Serving Love at Carnival
A Grand Prix Romance
An Ace in the Tiebreak

AN ACE IN THE TIEBREAK

Dedication

For Mary. Thanks for nagging us into this—hope you love it!

Chapter One

Robin couldn't restrain the curl to his upper lip as he opened the door to the light knock and met Danie Coetzee's smug expression. It immediately put his back up, never mind the fact that he was the one who had invited him there. Sort of.

"Oh, fuck you," he said by way of greeting, debating bouncing the steel hotel door off the other player's face. When Danie merely smirked at him from under his concealing hoodie, Robin grabbed his rival by the arm and yanked him into the room. "Idiot. Don't just stand there. Get in here before someone sees you." He slammed the door and crossed his arms. "Or leave. I don't care."

"*Howzit, brah*? Miss me?" The South African was unflappable as ever, and for some reason that pissed Robin off even more. "I got your text," he added unnecessarily. That much was obvious, otherwise Danie would have had no way of knowing where to come to follow through on the silent promise they'd exchanged earlier at the practice courts.

The top players kept out of the public eye as much as possible during the Grand Slams, and even though Robin's preferred hotel while in Paris—a small, family-run hotel off the Champs-Élysées—was fairly well known to those in the tennis world, Danie wouldn't have known what room he was in this year...which was why Robin had texted it to him earlier. Just that—nothing else. Nothing to tie them together.

Danie stripped off his jacket and hung it in the closet, then he sniffed at Robin and frowned, looking around the room. "Have you been drinking?"

Robin shrugged. "Just a little pick-me-up." He walked farther into the room, unconcerned about whether Danie followed him. "Quit nagging, *Mother*. You sound like my coach. And I can't believe you just hung up a sweatshirt." He picked up the glass and scooped ice into it by dipping it right into the half-full ice bucket then draining off the melted water. Before setting it down on the desk, he had to clear a spot as the remains of his *steak frites* and dessert still littered the surface. Noticing the Soma pill bottle sitting in plain view, he quickly moved the room service dome to cover it.

Danie came up behind him and grabbed his wrist as he reached for the vodka bottle. Against his will, Robin gave a little shudder of reaction. Danie wasn't overly bulky—no professional tennis player was—but he was taller and broader than Robin, and Robin knew he was more than capable of restraining him. The reason that sent a swell of anticipation to his cock was beyond him. Stupid thing.

"Why I need to remind you of this, I have no idea," Danie murmured in his ear, "but you have first round play tomorrow. You should not be drinking tonight.

You shouldn't be drinking at *all*, but the night before a match? Especially at Roland Garros?"

Robin refused to justify his scolding with a response but he didn't move away. He could feel the warmth radiating from Danie.

"You're pissing your career away. Makes it easier for me, so thanks for that. I'm looking forward to hoisting up La Coupe in a couple of weeks."

He tried to jerk away then. "Fuck off. You're a moose on clay. I certainly don't need to follow your 'clean living' ideals to wipe the court with you."

Danie tightened his grip on Robin's forearm and snaked his other arm around Robin's waist, tugging him fully back so Robin's ass was up against his evident erection.

"If you need something to self-medicate your issues with, I am more than happy to give you a much more enjoyable reason to be slow on your feet tomorrow."

His eyelids closed in response. When Danie finally released his wrist, Robin reached back and grabbed a handful of Danie's tight butt, holding him in place as he rubbed his ass along that tempting ridge. Hating himself for allowing Danie to put him in this position once again, Robin vowed — not for the first time — that this would be the last time he'd allow Danie in. He'd promised himself the same thing a month ago at the Italian Open, and look how that had gone. In reality, he knew full well that would only last until the next time Danie gave him that inquiring eyebrow in passing at some future tournament.

They were so unsuited for one another it was ridiculous. Sexual chemistry wasn't a problem between them, but they were direct competitors duking it out in the top ten world rankings of the professional tennis tour. Not only was fucking the enemy not wise from a mental game standpoint, if it was discovered it could end their careers...not to mention cost them their real bread and butter — endorsements.

The biggest barrier between them, though, was Danie's stinging disdain of Robin's lifestyle. The judgmental prick always managed to get his digs in when they were in private. In public, he threw down so very politely that most people took him as being a nice guy giving him his due, when Robin knew he was really being sarcastic and...and... Robin's eyes drifted closed as Danie ran the flat of his palm down over Robin's erection. He shut his brain off.

Time to get naked and get fucked. He ripped his shirt up over his head.

Danie's amazing reflexes kicked in and he moved just in time to avoid getting clobbered by Robin's elbow. He sat on the foot of the bed and started untying his shoes.

"I assume you brought stuff." Robin shimmied out of his sweatpants. No underwear tonight — he figured it would have been a waste of time.

"Just for assuming, I should say no." Danie was taking his sweet time getting out of his clothes, peeling his socks off like they'd break or something.

"Fuck off and give it to me." He stood in front of Danie and made gimme motions with his hand. He knew Danie would have brought supplies if only for the fact that he needed extra-large condoms. "I need to do a little work to take that extra leg you call a cock."

Danie snorted then gestured to the closet. "It's all in my jacket pocket."

After giving a loud sigh, Robin crossed the room to fumble through three pockets before he found the right one. When he turned around, he found Danie was down to just his jeans and had been staring at his ass. He didn't bother hiding the fact and kept his gaze on Robin's growing erection as Robin walked back across the room to the bed.

After throwing himself down, he tossed the strip of condoms to the side and used his teeth to crack open the stubborn flip top on the tube of slick. Danie stood and slowly undid the fastenings of his jeans while Robin made a quick job of lubing himself inside and out. He'd die before admitting that he'd already gotten himself mostly ready before Danie came over.

When Danie's pants hit the floor, Robin gave himself one more pass with his slicked fingers then tossed the closed tube in Danie's direction.

Danie wasn't a kisser—at least not with Robin. Robin knew that and he still felt a twinge of sadness as Danie moved over the top of him and sat back on his heels, giving Robin's shaft a few pumps with one hand while he tested Robin's entrance with fingers of the other. It wasn't that Danie was a selfish lover—it's just that they weren't 'lovers', and probably never would be. He sighed again.

"All ready? Okay?" Danie asked with a slight frown as he paused with his wrapped cockhead against Robin's hole.

"Yeah. Go."

As Danie pressed slowly inside, Robin's eyes closed. This was likely the most affection he'd ever see from Danie, though whether it was because he wasn't capable of it or that he thought Robin wasn't worthy of more, he didn't know. Maybe both.

But fuck, it was good.

They knew each other well enough to work steadily toward completion together. Close to the end Robin liked it hard, and Danie always obliged. He pulled out so he could flip Robin over then gripped his hips as he pushed back in, bringing them both to the brink of coming. The friction and angle had Robin gasping. He braced himself on the headboard and Danie reached under to give Robin's cock a few tugs — all he needed at that point to release the built up tension as he came with a groan.

Danie grasped his shoulder and gave a last volley of thrusts before stilling, his pubic hair rough against Robin's ass. Robin dropped his head to his forearms then turned his head to the side, wishing that Danie would lean down and kiss him. What he got was a light rub to his back and shoulders then Danie carefully withdrew. They took turns cleaning up.

Afterward, he brooded as he lay in bed and watched Danie dress in silence then walk to the hotel room door. He checked through the peephole before turning back to Robin.

"Put the vodka away and sleep it off." However it had been intended, Danie's words came out like an order that perversely made Robin want to do the opposite. "Good luck tomorrow," he added as he opened the door.

Robin didn't bother to answer. As soon as the door clicked shut, he got up, wincing at the ache in his ass and twinge in his knee. He picked up his glass, ice long melted into water. About to dump it into the ice bucket, he paused then found his Soma and swallowed two pills, draining the glass.

It wasn't until he was flipping on the bathroom light that he realized he'd automatically refilled the glass with vodka he didn't remember pouring.

Shrugging, he took a gulp, enjoying the burn as it went down, then turned on the shower.

Chapter Two

Eyes narrowed against the sweat dripping down his face, Robin rocked slowly from side to side as he waited through the big Serb's lengthy preparation to serve.

His first round opponent had a huge serve...when he got it in. It was the kid's biggest asset and at the same time his worst fault. His first serve percentage was one of the lowest on the tour, and thank God for that, because when he did get it in, he usually got an ace. Robin just couldn't seem to get into this match, but the double faults and softer second serves had kept him in it. Problem was, he was already two sets down — *two!*

In the first fucking round. How the hell had that happened?

The first set had been a disaster. He'd had his serve broken twice, while Stojanović had done better than usual, holding serve. The second set he'd warmed up a little and it had been a slug-fest, with both of them breaking serve once, ending up in a tiebreak that Robin had gone on to lose.

Now Robin was down a break in the third and if Stojanović held serve this game, he'd be one fucking game away from winning the match...and sending Robin home. The top seed, and his French might be over in the first round.

This isn't supposed to be happening.

He tried to keep panic from setting in and concentrate on taking it one point at a time. But it was hard to tune out the crowd, which had basically turned on him. His detractors were delighted and actively cheering against him, neutral spectators were excited about seeing a possible upset, and his fans were disappointed in him.

You'll never win if you don't fight for it. The voice in his head sounded a lot like Danie.

As soon as the ball was tossed, Robin went up onto his toes, trying hard as fuck to inject some spring, some energy into his play. It was as though gravity was working overtime today, slowing him down. The ball kicked out wide to his backhand and he lunged after it, barely managing to get a racquet on it. It just cleared the net, though with no momentum, but at least it was in play and Stojanović had to come in to the net. He got there and dug it off the clay just before it dropped dead, sending it deep crosscourt and catching Robin flat-footed. Knowing he had no chance of getting there in time, he helplessly watched it land inbounds as he conserved his energy and jogged to a halt before walking back toward the baseline.

"*Quarante, quinze.*" The chair umpire announced the score.

"Fuck," he muttered under his breath. "Come on. You should be in this. Come the fuck *on.*"

Robin accepted a towel from the ball girl, swabbed his face, neck and arms with it then tossed it back. He took his place behind the baseline and waited. This time fortune smiled on him and the serve, while fast, was flatter and didn't spin out. He brought his forehand through and painted a blistering return right down the sideline for the point.

"*Quarante, trente.*"

"Yes!" He gave a head jerk of mingled self-disgust and approval and crossed back to the other side of the court. He waved off the towel being held up, dried his racquet hand on his shorts instead and settled in to await the serve.

Stojanović had been kicking his ad side serves out wide all day, so when the serve came unexpectedly in toward his body, Robin scrambled to get his racquet in position and get his damn feet moving to carry his body out of the way. He punched it...short, into the net.

"*Jeu Stojanović.*"

Whistles broke out amidst the cheers for the Serbian kid. Jesus. This was getting ugly. Robin couldn't get over the fact that it was the first round and he was one measly game away from being out of the Grand Slam altogether. He hadn't been eliminated in first round play since... He shook his head. He couldn't actually remember when the last time had been. The whole match had been surreal, as though he was stuck in a nightmare where no matter how hard he tried, he couldn't make things go his way.

Hold serve. For God's sake, hold your fucking serve, Keller.

Robin repeated that mini-mantra over and over as he sorted through the balls to find the ones he preferred, shoved them into his pocket then accepted a towel. He approached the service line and pulled a ball back out then assessed Stojanović's position as he prepared to serve. He was shadowing to the forehand side, so he went inside.

"*Let!*" came from the chair umpire just before a lineman yelled "*Faute!*"

The umpire then announced in a voice he was rapidly coming to hate, "*Deuxième balle.*"

No shit.

He ground his teeth together. Just couldn't catch a break. After pulling the remaining ball out of his pocket, he adjusted his stance for his second serve and lollipopped it into play. As he'd expected, his opponent pounced on it and sent it winging back down the line. He'd already started moving in that direction and he slid easily on the clay as he got there and connected the ball with his backhand, putting it crosscourt for the point.

Yes.

On the next two points, though, his first serves went into the net and his second serves got pounded back down his throat. There was a lump in his throat blocking his air that he couldn't swallow down. Across the net, Stojanović definitely looked like he could taste victory, and instead of getting nervous, he was actually tightening up his game while Robin's fell apart.

"*Double balle de match Stojanović.*" Lots of cheers, jeers and whistles followed the announcement of double match point over the microphone. "*Silence, s'il vous plaît!*" the chair umpire admonished the crowd. "*Merci.*"

Robin let out a deep, blowing breath and rolled his shoulders, trying to keep a neutral expression on his face when all he wanted to do was wing his racquet into the stands. He pointedly avoided looking toward the box where his coach and manager were sitting.

None of his family were here to witness this—his parents only came for the second week at Roland Garros. He wondered randomly whether they could get a refund on their flight.

By now, he'd lost all confidence in his serve, so he just threw the ball up and served on total autopilot. To his shock, it went over the net into play—probably his best serve of the day. Even then, Stojanović's adrenaline must have been running wild because he met the ball perfectly and turned its momentum back around, sending it straight back at Robin.

As soon as his racquet connected with the ball, he knew. He didn't even have to watch it hit the net, didn't have to hear the call of *"Jeu, set, match Stojanović!"* from the chair, didn't have to hear the roar of the crowd and see the cameras going ballistic. Robin walked in a daze to the net where Stojanović was waiting to shake. He clasped hands with the grinning kid, who pulled him into a thumping hug over the net. They barely knew each other, but it was fine. Stojanović had probably seen the brackets and never imagined he'd survive to the second round—he had to be pumped.

"I am sorry," was whispered in his ear before they parted, and that caused the blockage in his throat to grow alarmingly. He managed a brief smile he was sure was more of a grimace. After shaking with the chair umpire, Robin strode over to his bench, threw his shit haphazardly into his bags then shouldered them both before freezing, gazing down at the racquet in his hand. As was his custom, he'd left it out to give to a lucky kid after the match, but now he feared he might not find one who would want it. It was too late to shove it into his already zipped bag, though, without drawing attention to himself.

He wasted little time in heading to the exit, leaving Stojanović on the court basking in the crowd's approval of his victory. He didn't blame him—he'd earned it. Robin scanned the crowd along the walkway, avoiding direct eye contact with anyone, and thankfully saw a young girl of around eight reaching grabby hands toward him. He stopped, stripped off his wristband and shoved it onto the handle of his racquet, then handed it to the girl, who was too excited to speak despite a woman's urging to thank him. He gave the child a genuine smile, the most he could manage anyway, then followed the usher toward the locker room.

By now Stojanović had caught up with him and entered the locker room just after he did. The players-only room was an oasis of quiet in the chaos and when the door closed, the relative silence was deafening.

Stojanović cleared his throat as though to get his attention, but Robin was in no mood to chat, so he pretended he didn't hear it and stripped off his soaked shirt. Stojanović seemed to get the hint and turned to rummage through his own belongings.

A few moments later, the door slamming open made them both jump, and Robin whipped around to meet Danie's irate face as he kicked the door shut behind him.

"What the utter fuck was that, Robbie?" Danie shouted, totally ignoring the presence of the other player as he rounded on Robin. "Did I or did I not tell you last night to get your head into why you're here? You looked like shit today. This has got to stop!" He didn't slow down as he headed straight into Robin's space.

Robin knew he would never hurt him, at least he thought as much, so he stood his ground until Danie actually chest-bumped him. Then he limited himself to taking one step back and resumed his defiant stance.

"Um…" Stojanović began.

Danie cut him off. "Shut it. Private matter."

"Fuck you—you can't talk to him like that." Robin seized upon anything else to fight about. "It's our locker room right now. You shouldn't even be in here. Who the fuck let you in?"

Danie gave him an exasperated look, and Robin let that go. Of course, with his ranking and credentials, he could go just about anywhere on the grounds and not be questioned.

"You're being rude," he continued, jabbing a finger at Danie then hastily putting it down when he realized it was noticeably trembling. "What are *you* so upset about anyway? I'm the one who fucking lost…" The last word came out strangled and to his utter horror, tears began to blur his vision. He blinked rapidly to try to keep them from falling.

He had nothing keeping him here—at Roland Garros, fuck, even in Paris. He wanted to go home. That thought echoed in his head, and he reminded himself that he *had* to go home now. No way did he want to hang around feeling the gleeful lenses of the paparazzi, and the no less intrusive sports reporters, on his every move.

He began to whirl around then Danie seized him by the arms with an iron grip. Robin winced as the hand on his right biceps pinched the skin. Danie gave a yank and all at once he was being held in those familiar, strong arms. Robin had no control over his reaction as he sagged into the rough embrace and gave into his shock at his loss. A jagged sob escaped him and he buried his face against Danie's chest.

After a couple of minutes of Robin embarrassing himself by leaking all over his rival's shirt, Danie's hold slackened and he awkwardly petted the back of Robin's head. "There, there, Robbie." His voice was a whisper, soft—very unlike how the pragmatic South African usually was with Robin. The tenderness caused a twinge in Robin's chest.

"It's not the end of the world. *But*," Danie added, his voice firming back up to his usual tone as he put Robin at arm's-length away from him, hands on his shoulders, "it might be the end of your *career* if you don't get your shit together." His gaze pierced Robin. "You have talent, but that won't amount to fuck-all if you piss your drive away with the crap you get up to. Yeah?" Danie's expression didn't invite anything except immediate agreement but Robin couldn't get any words out.

Danie seemed to understand and he nodded twice as he let go of him, then gave Robin's bare pec a double-tap with the flat of his hand. "I have to go. My warm-up slot starts in a few minutes. When are you leaving?"

Robin shrugged. He'd prefer to leave the country right now, but maybe he'd just hole up in his hotel room for a few days. He winced. He still had to face his coach and manager, and probably sit there for a really brutal press conference.

Fuck.

"Have to talk to Coach and Alfred still. I…" He shook his head. "Good luck on your match today," he changed the subject.

Danie narrowed his gaze. "Thanks, *brah*. Maybe I'll see you later?"

"Maybe I'll be around." That was all he was willing to commit to, because while he was still feeling the effects from last night's pounding, a part of him craved the escapism and body contact that Danie appeared to be offering. But did he really want to go there after such a crushing defeat, especially with the man who would likely win Le Coupe instead of him now that he was out?

Yeah—pretty much.

You are fucked in the head, Keller.

Danie looked him up and down, lingering for a moment on his nipples which tightened under the perusal. "Go take a shower before you get chilled." He turned and paused. Stojanović was staring at the two of them with the same shocked expression he'd had when Danie had come busting into the room. "Congratulations on your win. Be best if you followed it up with at least one more."

"Thank you. I mean, that is the plan, of course." Stojanović swallowed. Robin knew how he felt—those cold eyes could be intimidating as fuck.

Danie walked out without another word to either of them, and the air pressure in the room changed in his wake. As soon as the door closed, both of them, as though choreographed, sank to their respective benches.

"So..." Stojanović broke the silence.

Robin held up a hand but the guy either didn't notice or decided to disregard it.

"Coetzee is a very intense guy. I hope I do not have to play him. I mean, I wish to move forward and if he does not lose, I will have to play him, but—"

"Trust me—he's not a superhero. He can be beat." Robin was freezing now from the drying sweat in the relatively cool room, just like Danie had predicted. Fucker always had to be right about everything. He rummaged for his toiletry bag.

"Well, of course. You have beaten him. Um... You two seem...close."

Robin jerked his head up. *Oh, man.* Had they given themselves away? "We're rivals." When Stojanović gave him a slightly arched eyebrow, he clarified, "Friendly rivals. Sort of friends, in a competitive way."

God, shut up.

"It's okay. I can see that you two are more than you appear in public. But you do not have to say it to me. I understand." He shrugged nonchalantly.

Robin gaped at the kid. Too soon he realized that when he should have been denying it or getting pissed off, he'd been caught like a deer in the headlights. Shit, probably time for some damage control. He mentally scrambled for something to spout—anything to deflect the direction this was going, but Stojanović interrupted him by leaning forward.

"Just so you know, though, I like the women. I just thought I should tell you before the shower." He laughed, then grabbed his things and walked into the other room, leaving Robin stunned.

What a fucking bizarre day.

And it wasn't even half over yet. If thing happened in threes, what other crazy, life-changing shit was about to come at him?

Chapter Three

Quinn frowned at his phone where it sat ringing on the island counter in his kitchen. Why did it seem like every time he got in the middle of a touchy cooking experiment someone called him? Shrugging, he turned off the burner. He'd have to go back and try it again. After wheeling over, he snatched the offending phone off the granite before answering.

"Damaris," he barked while moving toward the sliding glass doors to the patio overlooking his backyard.

"Mr Damaris, I'm Alfred Stein. I'm interested in hiring you to cook for my client."

He rolled his eyes. Getting that kind of call wasn't surprising. Ever since he'd cooked for and helped DeShon Jefferson, the All-Pro wide receiver, got his diet back on track after his cancer diagnosis, Quinn had been approached by other agents and managers trying to get their own athletic stars in top shape. He tended to pick and choose his clients because of his own set of complications.

"Who is your client?" He returned to the small café table he'd put in his breakfast nook then made sure his laptop was connected to the internet while he waited for an answer.

"Robin Keller." Alfred seemed to be holding his breath after he said that, since there was a rather pregnant pause.

Keller? Why does that sound familiar? He would look the guy up later, wanting to hear what the manager had to say about him.

"I'm sorry. I've been on a retreat for the last week or so and haven't been anywhere near a TV or radio." Which was true as far as it went. He had been on a retreat where he'd limited his contact with the outside world. "Why do you want me to help you out?"

"Mr Keller is one of the top ten men's tennis players in the world, but ever since the Australian Open this year, he's been on a downward spiral. You were recommended to me by a colleague of mine. Your technique and diet plan worked miracles with his client." Alfred hesitated for a moment and Quinn jumped in.

"I don't mean to be a doubting Thomas or anything like that, but why do you think it's his diet that needs help? How do you know he's not drinking or abusing drugs? There are a lot of other things that can affect someone negatively that I can't help with." He wasn't a therapist, though he'd discovered that much like a bartender, a chef tended to be a confessional for his clients. Maybe it had something to do with how most people equated the kitchen with home and growing up. They remember spending time there watching Mom cook dinner and telling her of their day.

He snorted silently to himself, knowing he wasn't anyone's image of a maternal figure. Yet he'd become the confidant for quite a few of his clients. If he were to write a tell-all book, he could blow a lot of careers out of the water. Of course, he'd have to break all those nondisclosure agreements he'd signed. Having gone through his own troubles after the accident that had taken his legs, Quinn had no interest in destroying someone else's life.

He stared down at where his legs ended just at the edge of his wheelchair. Yesterday had been spent on his feet all day and his stumps ached from using his prosthetic legs for that long. So he'd decided to not use them when he woke up that morning.

Alfred sighed. "I know he probably has more problems that need to be addressed, but at the moment, I want to start with his diet and training regime. His coach has him doing all his practice and things like that and I know that's helping him stay relatively focused."

"You think that with a new diet and maybe me getting him to add other activities to his training, he'll come around without you having to do a bigger intervention," Quinn said.

"Yes. I'd prefer there not be any publicity about this whole thing."

"I'd be willing to sign a confidentiality clause if you want, but I'm not saying I'll take the job. You do know that I present my own set of challenges to this. I'm assuming you'd like me to be a live-in chef for a while—or at least until we get him on the road to winning again."

Alfred cleared his throat. "I am aware of your situation, Mr Damaris, and it won't be a problem. There's a small suite just off of the kitchen at Mr Keller's house that you can use. It and the kitchen are all on the same level, along with the weight room my client had installed when he bought the place. There are two steps leading down into the living room. If you agree to the contract and come to Switzerland, I would be more than willing to remodel anything that you needed done once you got here."

"What about Keller? Will he be as willing? Does he even know what you're up to?" It wouldn't be the first time Quinn had been dropped like a bomb into someone's life. Didn't mean he liked it, though.

"After his dismal performance at the French, he doesn't get any say in this." Alfred sounded determined.

Quinn rolled his eyes. It always seemed like coaches, trainers and managers thought they controlled the relationship with the athletes and actors they worked with. But he'd found that the one making the most money called the shots.

"Where does Keller live?" He needed to know how big a trip it was going to be and how long he was going to be gone. "And how long do you want me to stay?"

"I think we'll do a three-month trial period. If it looks like your process is working, I'd like you to sign on for another nine months. An entire year from now through next year's French. Hopefully Robin will have done better than he did this year." Alfred grunted. "He lives in Lucerne, Switzerland. Would you be interested, Mr Damaris?"

Switzerland. He'd never been to the mainland of Europe. He'd spent some time in England and Scotland, but at times traveling was difficult for him and he just didn't have the energy to go. Yet he wouldn't be traveling much once he got to Keller's home. He would be living there, so it wouldn't be as much trouble as before.

"It's going to take me a week or two to get packed and fly over," he said.

"I'll charter you a plane. That'll make it easier for you since I can't think it's comfortable for you to fly commercial." Relief colored Alfred's voice.

Quinn bit his tongue to keep from saying something snarky because the man was right. Flying coach wasn't comfortable, whether he had his legs on or not. He usually wore them to get on the plane instead of using his wheelchair, just to keep from having to deal with the needing help shit. "That would be helpful."

"But I need you here before that. Is there any way you can get here sooner than that?"

"I guess I could have someone else close up my place for me," he muttered then thought about it. His mind went to Morgan who had called him earlier in the day, asking if he could come crash with him for a while. He could let Morgan stay and watch the place, though if he decided to leave, Quinn would have to find someone else take care of his house. "Give me your number and I'll call you tomorrow when I figure out some arrangements."

"Thank you. I do appreciate you dropping everything you're doing to help me and Robin. I have to admit he's probably not going to be happy about it, but I don't care. I believe in him and he needs to get his head out of his ass before he loses everything he worked so hard for." Alfred gave him his personal number. "I'll send you the contract terms, so you can decide if it's worth it. Then I'll make the arrangements as soon as you call."

"Thank you, Mr Stein." He hung up then dropped his phone in his lap while he went online to search out all the information he could find on Robin Keller.

A few hours later, he sighed as he shut off his laptop. Quinn moved around the kitchen, cleaning up the meal he'd been in the middle of cooking when Stein called. Once those dishes were taken care of, he started pulling other ingredients out so he could make his favorite pie—key lime. Quinn rarely ate dessert. It has hard for him to keep weight off without working out like crazy and eating healthy was the best way for him to do it, though he did indulge once in a while.

Once the pie was in the oven, he picked up his phone and punched in Morgan's number, putting it on speaker. He went to the refrigerator to pull out a beer.

"What's up, Ace?" Morgan's voice came over the line.

"Are you somewhere you can talk for a little bit?" He'd heard a bunch of noise in the background. "What's going on?"

"Just blowing off a little steam, but I'll go outside."

The noise disappeared then he heard a bang as though Morgan had let a door slam shut behind him.

"How was your last mission?" He usually didn't ask about Morgan's work because most of it was classified. But his brother and his team didn't get loud when they came back unless something had happened.

"It was better than some and worse than others." Morgan's answer was suitably ambiguous and Quinn wasn't interested in asking for more detail.

"Sorry to hear that." He took a sip of his beer then said, "I know you said you would be showing up some time next week, but I was wondering if you might be able to come earlier."

"I'd have to clear it with my superior, but I have a ton of leave stored up and I'm done with my debriefing, so I don't see why not. What's up?"

"I got a job offer in Lucerne, Switzerland and they want me there as soon as possible. It might end up being for a year, so you can stay at my place for as long as you want." He would've offered that anyway, but knowing his brother would be hanging out would make him feel better.

"Thanks. I need a place away from here to give me a chance to clear my head and think about things. I might have to go on missions before you get back."

Quinn nodded, even though he knew Morgan couldn't see him. "I know. I have friends who can check on the place when you're away, or if you know anyone who could come and stay that would be fine as well."

"No problem, Ace. I know a couple guys who need a place to crash after missions. Places where they won't be bothered by anyone."

He smiled at the nickname Morgan had given him when they were little. "Well, you really can't get much more quiet than my place."

Which was what made it the perfect home for him. He could go days without seeing another human, since his house sat at the top of a mountain in Colorado. During the winter, he got snowed in and he was happy about that. Before his accident, he'd been an extreme sports enthusiast, spending all his time traveling to different areas of the world. He had a ton of friends and rarely stayed at his place for longer than a week.

Yet after he was let out of the hospital and rehab facility, he'd come back to his home and discovered he loved the silence and remoteness. Morgan had renovated it to suit his needs, making sure Quinn could get around with his wheelchair and prosthetics when he wore them. It had taken him a few months to get used to the quiet, plus adjusting to relearning his space with a wheelchair.

Morgan had been a great help, but he couldn't stay forever, so when he'd left, Quinn had dug deep and found out that he was strong enough to go on. He couldn't do all the sports he'd done before he lost his legs, but he participated in new ones. Yet he wasn't on the go like he had been. He'd discovered the peace of silence and meditation, deciding not to look back on what his life had been like before he sacrificed his legs to the whims of Mother Nature.

"I'll talk to my superiors then call you back about the time I'll be getting to your place," Morgan told him. "Is the job going to be worth it?"

"I'll know by the time you call me, but I'm pretty sure it will be. Plus I'll be able to visit a country I've never been to before. It was on my list to climb the Alps before I got too old to do it. It's too late for me to do that now."

"True in so much as you can't really climb any mountains on your own because it'll take some planning to do." Morgan paused for a second as though he were thinking then continued, "Maybe when your contract is up with this client, we can go climbing. I'll have to look into it."

"Thanks, Morgan."

"No big deal, Ace. I've been wanting to spend some time with you and helping you cross something off your bucket list would be pretty cool. You know, that list can't have too many things on it. You were having a lot of adventures before you lost your legs."

"There isn't, but I'm thinking that after this contract is over and we do our Alps thing, I'm going to head down to the Guadalupe Islands and dive with sharks." He grinned at the thought.

"I might join you for that adventure as well." Morgan grunted. "I better get back to the guys. I'll give you a shout tomorrow to let you know for sure when I'm getting in. If you need to leave before I get there, that's cool."

Quinn said, "Thanks, bro. I'll talk to you later."

"Bye, Ace."

After hanging up, he set the phone on the counter before finishing his beer. Then he rolled out onto his patio, staring out over the forest spread in the valley below him. As he studied the scene, he took deep breaths and let his mind slowly go blank. He didn't want to think about any option or decision he had to make. All he wanted was to calm his heartbeat and relax.

No matter what, whether he went to Switzerland or not, he'd be fine. The worst that could happen to him had already come to pass. Helping a man get his life back on track couldn't be harder than learning how to walk again.

Chapter Four

As the car turned into the driveway, Quinn swore under his breath. Apparently Keller lived in a castle — all stone and turrets. The windows were deep set in the weathered walls, and large wooden doors barred entrance into the house. *Who built this place? Some minor prince in the fourteen hundreds or something?*

When the driver stopped the limo, Quinn took a deep breath. *Why am I nervous? I've had other clients who had houses bigger than this one and who have probably made far more money than Keller has. There's no reason to be freaked out by this place.*

"How can this place be modern enough to be easy for me to get around in?" he muttered under his breath as he slid out of the vehicle. He braced his hand on the roof until he was sure he had his balance. "Thanks."

Quinn took his carry-on from the driver before making his way slowly over the gravel path leading up to the front steps. Pausing, he took a deep breath then gripped the railing.

"Wait."

Glancing up, he spotted a short rather pudgy man in a sweater vest striding toward him. "Mr Stein?"

"Yes. There's a ramp over to the left that will bring you up to the landing. I didn't want to ruin the look of the facade, so I had them put it in behind the hedges over here." Stein gestured to his left and when Quinn turned in that direction, he spotted the new wooden ramp tucked discreetly behind the bushes there.

"God forbid we ruin the look of the castle," he murmured while walking over to it. As much as he wanted to say something louder for Stein to hear, he bit his tongue. There'd been nothing in the contract that stated a ramp had to be put in for him. He could've climbed the stairs, even though it would've taken him a while.

"Here. Let me take that." Stein grabbed Quinn's bag and tugged.

Quinn tightened his grip, glaring at the man. "I can get it. Listen, Stein. I'm only going to say this once. If I need help, I'll ask for it. Until then, just assume I can do it for myself. You're not going to be around all the time while I'm cooking and trying to clear your client's head. Unless you don't think I can do the job."

Stein stuttered as he let go of the bag.

"If you thought that, why did you hire me?" As he stared at Stein, he continued up the ramp to where it leveled out.

Stein cleared his throat. "I'm sorry. I just haven't dealt with a…"

"An amputee?" He paused, not really wanting to pursue the conversation. He hated being treated like he couldn't do things people with their natural legs could do.

"Sir? Where would you like me to put your bags and chair?" The driver met them at the front door.

"Am I staying, Stein? If I do, you have to forget the fact that I wear fake legs when I stand upright." Quinn lifted his eyebrows in a silent question.

"Yes, you're staying. Just put those things in the foyer. Mr Keller's maid will put them away." Stein shoved open the enormous wooden door before motioning for them to follow him.

Quinn snorted quietly. "Of course he has a maid. He can't be counted on to take care of himself or his home," he said under his breath, then louder, he asked, "Have you told Keller that he'll be getting a personal chef and babysitter?"

"No. He'll be arriving home today and I'll talk to him then about this whole thing. He has to know we'll be stepping in to change the path he's been taking. We didn't work this hard and long for him to throw his career away." Stein scowled.

"Don't you mean *he* didn't work this hard to throw it all down the drain?" He stumbled slightly as he caught his foot on the threshold but remained standing without making a complete idiot of himself.

"I'm not going to debate that with you, Mr Damaris. I'm sure you're probably tired. I'll show you to your suite and you can get some rest. When you wake, I'll have the maid show you around the house and the kitchen. You'll also give me a list of food you want to start Robin on. I'll make sure it gets delivered." Stein met Quinn's gaze with a determined expression on his face.

"You're right. I need to rest for a little while." It was more he needed to take his legs off for a few hours because his stumps were starting to ache. "I'm going to hold off on making that list for you until I've talked to Keller. Ultimately, it's his decision whether I stay. Not yours."

Stein didn't reply, just continued on through the house and while Quinn would've liked to look around, his traveling was catching up to him. He could feel exhaustion weighing him down and his coordination was getting worse.

They made their way straight through the kitchen, and he decided he'd give himself a tour of the room later. When he was living in, he liked to learn the place where he'd be cooking without interference from anyone. Of course, something told him Keller didn't spend a lot of time in the kitchen. Hell, he probably didn't spend a lot of hours in his entire house.

"Here's your suite. There's a small sitting room. Your bedroom is to the right and your private bath is to the left. If you want the weight room, continue down this hall to the end where you'll find the pool and workout area." Stein glanced into the room. "I see your bags sitting on the bench at the end of your bed. I'll leave you to rest and will talk to you later."

Quinn rolled his eyes at Stein's retreating back before he strolled into the sitting area. It was sunny from the big windows overlooking a flower garden and felt homey. Once he got into the bedroom, he didn't even pay attention to what it looked like. All he was interested in was the queen-sized bed.

"I hope it's comfortable," he commented as he sat on the edge of the mattress.

He had to call Morgan and let him know he'd made it to the house. Morgan had insisted on getting the international service added to Quinn's phone, telling him he'd pay for it. It was worth it for the peace of mind it would give Morgan, knowing Quinn could call him at any time. Quinn could've been insulted by Morgan's protective nature, thinking it had to do with his challenges, but he knew it simply came from Morgan being his older brother.

As he dug his phone out of his duffle, he glanced down to where his feet hung a few inches above the floor. Before his accident, he hadn't had to worry about touching the floor. But the doctors had taken an inch or two extra when they'd removed his legs to be able to give him the best and smoothest amputation sites. At least they'd only had to do it below the knee. He wasn't sure how he would've dealt if he didn't have those.

Still not being able to reach the floor—even with his prosthetics—made him feel like a little kid at times. It was also why he took a minute to get his balance when he stood.

He punched Morgan's number on the speed dial then flopped back to look up at the ceiling. It was painted a pleasing light blue with white swirls that looked like clouds. Wiggling slightly, he smiled. The bed felt like it would be comfortable to sleep on.

"Hey, Ace, you get there okay?" Morgan's voice came over the speaker and eased the rest of Quinn's tension.

"Yeah. Just got to my suite. I'm going to take a nap. Jet lag's hit me pretty hard, but I wanted to let you know I'm here." He pushed himself upright.

"Met the big guy yet?"

"No. I guess he's coming in later. He doesn't know I'm going to be here, so that should be interesting." He grimaced. "I hate scenes like that. Why can't these managers, agents and coaches ever think that maybe they don't know what's best for their clients. Or at least get their permission before they hire someone."

Morgan snorted. "Because they're all egomaniacs, bro. They know everything. Hit the hay and call me tomorrow. Doesn't matter what time. I probably won't be sleeping anyway."

He wasn't happy to hear that. Something had happened during Morgan's last mission that seemed to be forcing his brother into making some life-altering decisions. He hated being on the other side of the world while Morgan was going through it.

"I will. Take care, Morgan."

"You too, Ace."

After ending the call, Quinn set his phone on the nightstand next to the bed before standing. Once he'd got his balance, he unbuckled his belt then unzipped his jeans. He shoved them down to just below his knees where his prosthetics started. He released his stumps—one at a time—from the sockets then eased further back on the mattress. Getting his jeans untangled from the fake legs took a few minutes, but he finally managed to do that and set them aside. Then he took the time to remove the stockings he used to protect and cushion the ends of his legs.

Quinn pulled a small bottle of lotion from his duffle to rub over the surgery scars. They weren't red or irritated, which sometimes happened when he wore his legs for long periods of time. He finished by stripping his T-shirt off, tossing it on the chair with his pants.

It always took some maneuvering, but he got himself under the blankets and situated in such a way that his legs wouldn't ache when he woke up. Taking a deep breath, he made a conscious decision to relax and worry about everything later. He shoved any worries he might have out of his mind, knowing it would be the only way he could sleep.

If Keller vetoes me being here, at least I got to come to Switzerland. Maybe I could convince Morgan to come out and spend some of his vacation with me. With that thought, Quinn allowed his exhaustion to sweep him under into sleep.

Chapter Five

At least he'd been spared Stein's company on the trip home. Robin glanced sideways at his way-too-quiet coach next to him in the backseat of the hired car. Something was up. Other than reviewing his usual area-by-area observations on his less-than-impressive play the day after the match he'd lost, he'd been silent on the topic of his loss. Robin had been expecting to get reamed.

Was it weird that he was disappointed he wasn't getting beaten down so he could fight back? He'd had the rug ripped out from under him at Roland Garros, and now his team was tiptoeing around him like he was on life support. He shifted in the limo seat, his chest constricting.

Did they not care anymore…because they were done with him? Were they planning to jump ship?

Fuck. He swallowed hard, pissed off at himself that he even cared. But it had been one bizarre thing after another for him to deal with this week—he was exhausted and not his usual self.

The interviews after the match had been brutal. It had actually been a tough Open for a lot of the top seeds this year, but a past champion going out in the first round had given the reporters a ton of ammunition. Thinking about Danie watching the interview sometime after his match was over, he'd swallowed his pride and tried to be as self-effacing and gracious as possible, when really he'd just wanted to punch someone. He'd been holding on by a thread when he'd finally gotten back to the privacy of his room to drown his sorrows. Well, maybe not drown — he'd only had less than half a bottle of vodka left and hadn't wanted to take the chance of calling attention to himself by going out or sending out for more.

So he'd been just drunk enough to answer the knock when his nemesis had shown up.

He'd already mentally prepared himself for certain expectations from Danie's visit. Still a bit tender from being fucked the night before, he knew he'd really be feeling it after that night.

Self-flagellation much?

Not so much, as it had turned out. Danie had evidently said all he'd wanted to say in the changing room earlier that day. He'd merely stripped down to his boxer briefs, climbed into bed and told him to get ready for the night.

When Robin had come out of the bathroom naked, Danie had lifted an eyebrow at him then raised the covers to invite him in. He'd completely thrown Robin for a loop when instead of instigating anything sexual, he'd just flicked the covers up over them both, tugged a stiff Robin up against him and closed his eyes.

They'd never slept together before that night. And to be honest, Robin hadn't slept much that night either. He'd had way too much spinning through his head —

his loss, Danie's odd behavior, the relentless downward slide he seemed to have been in since Australia. He'd eventually relaxed and drifted off and when he'd finally woken to the sound of his phone the next morning, Danie had been gone.

Even though Robin had hung around in Paris for another week, he hadn't spoken to Danie since then. Of course, the South African had been busy with his own play in the Open. He'd eventually lost to Nadal in the quarters and afterwards headed to the home he kept in Monaco for the short break before the next tournament in Germany. Not that Robin cared enough to keep tabs on Danie, but Danie had texted to let him know he was leaving Paris and wanting to know if he'd see Robin in Halle.

The Gerry Weber Open was an ATP grass court tournament that many players used as a run-up to Wimbledon. Even though Robin was obviously entered, he understood why Danie had asked, as Robin had withdrawn from it more often than he'd played. Grass wasn't his best surface, and he was always exhausted after the French since he usually went at least as far as the semis.

He didn't have that excuse this year, but still hadn't decided whether he wanted to play. God knows he didn't want to show his face after his humiliation at Roland Garros — and his coach and manager hadn't mentioned a word about it, when usually they'd be all over planning for the next tournament.

The lack of reaction made him nervous. And his overall lack of confidence was starting to really freak him out. It ran counter to his whole personality and the drive that had gotten him to where he was.

He really needed a drink.

Just as it became dark enough to need headlights, they pulled up to the gated entrance of his home and he slumped with relief. In just a few minutes he could get rid of Coach—and probably Stein too, since there was a hired car sitting in the drive, damn it—and hole up in privacy until he got his head screwed back on straight.

Coach Ramsey touched his arm as they came to a halt. "Don't disappear. We need to have a conversation now that we're here."

And here it comes.

"Yes, Coach," he answered automatically, though he still planned to do his own thing the second he got inside. It was his damn house, and if they thought he was going to sit there and allow them to rip him to shreds, they had another think coming.

Ramsey obviously saw right through his meaningless agreement because his lips twisted into a wry smile. "Don't worry. It's a good thing we've put into motion. Just hear us out."

Robin nodded absently and got out of the car before his words really registered. Wait. 'Put into motion'? What the hell did that mean?

Coach was already striding toward the front door, which opened to reveal his manager.

Surprise, surprise.

A closer look as he approached the door revealed that Stein looked...nervous? The man was nothing if not confident, so seeing him looking a bit worried had more of an effect on Robin than if they'd come at him guns blazing. What the hell was he in for? His coach stopped just to the side of the door, so he'd have to pass right between the two of them.

"Robin. Welcome home. Could you come in and have a seat, please? We'd like to have a strategy meeting with you."

Rolling his eyes at the absurdity of being invited into his own house, Robin cruised past them and continued down the entry hall without turning toward the living room. "Later. I'm tired."

"Robin." His coach's voice stopped him in his tracks. Occupational hazard of having been under the tutelage of the man since he weighed less than one hundred pounds. "Please. This conversation needs to happen right now. We're not trying to be assholes, but there are reasons it's urgent."

He sighed. "Fine." Backtracking to the living room, he glanced between the two men, his discomfort increasing with every moment that passed. He threw himself down on the sofa, crossed his arms then forced himself into a less defensive posture. The other men took their seats and looked at each other.

Coach went first. "Something needs to change. Your ranking is slipping, your endurance is for shit and even the parts of your game that have always been excellent are subpar. Most damaging, though, is your mental game." He shook his head. "You're just not focused on what you need to do."

"So we've had to make a difficult decision," Stein continued, all businesslike.

That was never good. Robin tensed and switched his focus from Ramsey to his clenched hands on his thighs.

"We're pulling you from most of your tournaments for the next three months in order to concentrate on getting you healthy and bringing your game back up to speed."

It was so far from the 'we quit' he'd expected to hear that it took him a few moments to process what Stein had actually said. He did some mental math. "Three months? And what do you mean 'some'? Not Wimbledon and the US Open, of course." He read the answer on Stein's face and turned to his coach, furious. "No fucking way! You are not pulling me out of the majors. It's *my* career. My *life*." He jumped to his feet and loomed over Stein. "You try it and I'll...I'll sue. You can't do that." Could they? *Fuck.*

A hand came down firmly on his shoulder. "Calm down, Robin. Some of this is negotiable...based on how cooperative you are in making changes. You have to agree that if this streak continues, you aren't going to have much of a career left. I'm sorry to say that, but it's a fact." Ramsey turned him around and stared into his eyes. "You are one of the most talented players I've ever seen. But right now, that player isn't showing up to matches. We are not giving up on you. Okay? We just want to turn things around. Do you?"

"Of course I do." His answer sounded trite and weak and defensive to his own ears. Thankfully his coach didn't call him on it.

"All right then." Ramsey glanced at Stein then stepped back and released Robin. He gestured to the coach and Robin obediently sat back down, his head spinning.

"We've hired Quinn Damaris, a live-in chef and...personal life coach, I suppose you'd call him," Stein announced. "He's very good at what he does and he's saved the careers of more than one professional athlete."

Robin frowned. *A live-in chef? Life coach? What the hell?* He opened his mouth to argue but his coach cleared his throat. Pressing his lips together, he swallowed his outburst.

"Quinn will be living here and managing your diet, and to a lesser extent your training schedule, in conjunction with Coach Ramsey. What we're asking from you is to follow his guidelines and advice with an open mind. If you do, you're almost guaranteed to see improvement in your overall health and, we hope, your game."

His coach added, "And if that's the case, we can keep you in the Grand Slam events."

It looked as though Stein wanted to argue with that, but Ramsey stared him down. A slight burst of warmth for the older man penetrated Robin's overwhelming swirl of emotions. Stein was clearly in it for the paycheck, but his coach had a soft spot for Robin, something he'd manipulated more than once. Refusing to acknowledge the shaft of guilt, he pulled himself up, trying to project confidence as he searched for an answer.

"I don't know about the 'life coach' bit—I'm a grown ass man—but I suppose having a chef would be okay. If he stays out of my way when I'm home."

"You two can work out the details of how it will work when he wakes up." Stein delivered that as he stood, Ramsey following suit.

"Wait…he's *here*?" That was not a screech, but a little too close for Robin's dignity.

"Yes, in the living quarters off the kitchen, and he's jet-lagged from his flight from the States, so keep it down," Stein chastised him. "He'll probably sleep until morning at this point." He walked at a rapid pace toward the front door, looking like a man who was trying to escape.

Ramsey lingered for a moment. "We're doing this for your sake, Robin. You know that, right?"

He set aside his irritation and shock at his life being hijacked and met his coach's worried gaze. "Yeah. I guess."

"Good." He slapped Robin on the back. "Remember — keep an open mind. What we're doing now obviously isn't working." Robin didn't miss the fact that Ramsey took the blame upon himself too. "We've put a lot of trust into Quinn's abilities, and I know you have what it takes to get it back. Don't worry — we'll play it by ear. We won't withdraw from any of the big tournaments yet."

But if there wasn't improvement, they would. That went unsaid but Robin heard it, loud and clear.

* * * *

Flipping through the channels didn't produce anything interesting to watch, which didn't really surprise Robin since it was a ridiculous time at night — nearly morning. In fact, the sky was starting to lighten and the birds were already doing their best to wake up the rest of the world. He rolled his head to the side to look at the wall clock. Four-thirty. Ugh.

Robin turned the TV in the game room off with the remote, then stretched hard…and almost slid right off the leather couch. Recovering, he scowled at the empty glass on the end table. He could go for one more vodka rocks before bed…but he had no rocks. He snickered a bit at the thought and debated for all of a minute before he levered himself to his feet, grabbed the glass and started to make his way downstairs.

He reached the kitchen and was about to push the glass against the ice dispenser of the fridge when he caught movement out of the corner of his eye.

"Shit!" The glass almost slipped out of his grasp and he barely kept it from crashing to the floor. Suddenly, he remembered about the new live-in chef-cum-babysitter. What was his name again? He went ahead and filled the glass with ice while he thought.

"Sorry. I didn't mean to startle you. Robin, right?"

The man spoke in English. He was a bit taller than average, though several inches shorter than Robin, and very muscular. His arms and chest were those of a man who devoted a lot of time to lifting weights. He was wearing a T-shirt that strained across his upper torso, then hung loose to where the hem covered the waistband of his pajama pants. No pot belly there.

Robin came back to himself just as his gaze began to drift below the waist and he made sure he returned his entire attention to the man's face. He was usually much better at keeping himself from checking guys out, but evidently the slight buzz he had had lowered his inhibitions.

"Are you okay? Do you speak English?" A pause. "Do you sleepwalk?"

Giving a burst of laughter at the latter question, Robin finally regained his equilibrium. "Yes. I mean, no. And yes. Wait..." He mentally sorted through the various questions. "Yes, I'm Robin and I'm fine. And no, I don't sleepwalk, that I know of anyway." He shifted the glass to his left hand and held out his right.

The man stepped forward and shook but didn't go along with the cue to introduce himself, forcing Robin to confess, "Um... Coach and Alfred told me you were here, but I'm sorry, I'm really bad with names..."

The man rolled his eyes. "Oh, of course. Quinn Damaris."

"That's right. My new watchdog." The pronouncement fell with an awkward thud into the quiet of the kitchen.

Quinn's eyebrow rose, his only reaction, and damned if it wasn't exactly the same expression that Danie would give him. Thinking of Danie and what his reaction to how he was acting would be made his next words a bit defensive. "Hey, nothing personal, but seriously—I get home and you're here and they tell me I have no choice but to put up with you or they'll pull me..."

He trailed off, not knowing the guy and really not wanting to give him any ammunition if he was the vindictive type. This was not going well. Time for a tactical retreat before he fucked it up even more.

"I just wanted some ice...water. I'm going to bed. Goodnight, or morning, or whatever time zone you're in." Robin whipped around and the world swam just a touch before he caught his balance. He strove for dignity as he aimed himself toward the living room and beyond that, the staircase.

"Goodnight, Robin. Sleep well and we'll talk more later."

That promise, or threat, echoed in his ears as he climbed the stairs. Man—his failings had just got real in a hurry.

Chapter Six

After drying off then dressing, Quinn ignored his legs as he swung himself into his chair before wheeling out of his room. He'd woken up around four-thirty and had gone for a walk about the house, trying to get the lay of the land. He'd even chatted with Robin for about five minutes before the guy had staggered off to bed.

Quinn shook his head at the knowledge that Robin had been drinking. He might not drink even to get a buzz anymore, but Quinn still remembered what having a little too much looked like. It was something that would have to be addressed when they discussed Robin's new diet plan.

Once Robin had left, he'd gone back to his suite where he'd decided to clean up after his travels. Now it was time for some meditation and to get ready to face his new client again. He headed down the hallway to where the weight room was, but turned to roll outside. Smiling, he lifted his head to soak up the early morning sunlight shining down onto the flagstone patio. He'd discovered this secluded area of the backyard earlier when he woke up, after having slept the night away. He was going to claim it as his meditation spot.

Usually he'd spread a towel on the ground and do some stretching before he meditated for thirty minutes, but today he stayed in his chair. Quinn cleared his mind and evened out his breathing. As he let his eyes drift close, he slowly began to relax each muscle group until all the aches that came from sleeping in certain positions to compensate for not having his lower legs were gone.

Thirty minutes later, he blinked, letting go of the last of his trance. He heard a noise behind him as the door opened. Swinging his chair around, he saw Robin standing in the doorway.

"What the fuck?" Robin stared at him. "You're a fucking cripple? Stein didn't tell me that."

Charming. "From what I understood yesterday, Stein and your coach haven't told you much of anything about me." He clenched his hands on the arms of his chair to keep from tugging on the hem of his shorts. He wanted to hide his stumps from Robin's gaze, which was a reaction he hadn't had in years.

"True, but you could've said something when we talked last night," Robin accused as he stepped out onto the patio.

Quinn frowned. "Why would I do that when I thought Stein had told you? I put my legs on instead of using my wheelchair then because I wanted to see your house. I needed to check to see where I'd be able to go if I choose not to wear them."

Robin glared at him for a moment before moving his gaze to one of the small fountains in the middle of the gardens. He could tell the tennis player was struggling not to yell at him or in his direction. Quinn was intelligent enough to know Robin's anger wasn't with him, and to be honest, most of it wasn't directed at Stein or his coach. His anger seemed focused on himself.

"Is there anything that needs to be remodeled for you?" Robin's voice was gruff as he asked.

"Not really. I'm going to need a bench for my shower, but I can order one and have it delivered. Other than that, I can get around the ground floor without a problem."

"What about upstairs?"

Quinn shook his head. "I won't go up there unless you give me permission or I think you're cheating on the rules I'm going to give you."

Robin snorted in disbelief. "Rules? Am I a five year old who needs a babysitter and rules?"

Fighting back a sigh, Quinn propelled his chair toward Robin, wondering if he was going to get out of the way. Robin stepped to the side just before Quinn hit him. Once he'd rolled inside, he twisted to look at Robin.

"I'll be making breakfast in thirty minutes. You are welcome to join me so that we can discuss what's going to happen for the next year, or you can continue being an ass, and go sulk in your room." He took a deep breath, trying to remind himself that his presence had been a shock for Robin and the man had the right to be upset. "I'm not here to be your babysitter, Mr Keller. I'm here to help you get as healthy as you possibly can be. I'm not interested in rankings or winnings. I am interested in you being in top physical shape."

He headed back down the hallway to his room where he quickly changed into his legs, jeans, and a T-shirt. He'd figured out that he wasn't going to be able to use his wheelchair in the kitchen. The counters weren't low enough for him, but he could work with it. Quinn never demanded any of his clients renovate their homes just because he was coming to stay with them for a while.

Quinn shut the door behind him then walked carefully along the smooth wooden floor to the kitchen. He didn't acknowledge Robin when the man entered the room then sat on one of the stools at the island counter.

"Can I have a cup of coffee?" Robin asked.

Motioning to the coffee maker, Quinn nodded. "Sure. How many cups would you say you drink a day?"

"What makes you think I drink a lot of it?" After standing, Robin moved around him to get a cup from the cupboard and filled a large mug.

"Hmm...maybe the size of your cups and the amount of sugar you're pouring into it." Quinn eyed his client for a second before turning back to gather the ingredients he needed to make waffles. There was fruit in the refrigerator as well.

"I'm going to have to go grocery shopping," he muttered as he set the milk and flour on the counter.

"Why? Isn't the kitchen stocked?" Robin frowned. "I pay someone to come and make sure there's food for me when I get back home."

Quinn shook his head. "You have ton of stuff, but it's not right for the diet you're going to be following for the next year."

Robin curled his upper lip. Quinn could see he wanted to say something, yet didn't. Either Robin had figured out that taking his anger out on Quinn wasn't going to work or he'd just decided it wasn't worth yelling at him again.

"While we're eating, I want to talk to you about what you eat and drink throughout the day. I'm sure you drink way more alcohol than you should."

Robin started to protest and Quinn held up his hand to stop him.

"Don't lie. I've seen and done it all myself. I know what a hangover looks like, plus earlier this morning I could tell you'd had a few too many. I spent a lot of time drowning my sorrows after I lost my legs." He chuckled. "And having a few drinks with friends before the accident."

"Is that what caused the accident?" Robin inclined his head toward Quinn's legs.

"Nope. We didn't do any of our shit while we were drunk or high. Hell, I was an adrenaline junkie. Anything dangerous or scary, I'd do, but we weren't into killing ourselves. We were all crazy assholes. Not stupid though." He began to mix the ingredients together. "Why don't you dig through your cupboards and find your waffle iron? I'm sure you probably have one, even if you've never used it."

Robin stuck out his tongue and Quinn laughed. He didn't continue with his story while he put together a breakfast that was low in calories, but still tasted good. Of course, it had gluten, something he was going to start weaning Robin off. Quinn only ate it occasionally now since his body didn't really deal with it well any more.

"Here you go. To be honest, I didn't even know I had one of these." Robin set the iron next to him on the counter. "My mom got me everything she said I needed for this place when I bought it. I was busy on the tournament circuit or something."

"How long have you lived here?" He sprayed the iron then poured some batter in the middle before he closed the top. While it cooked, he chopped up the fruit.

"About five years now." Robin glanced around the kitchen. "The only parts of this entire place that feel like home are my bedroom and the tennis court out back. I'm usually not here long enough to mess it up or anything."

Quinn grunted, choosing to keep his opinion to himself at the moment. "What made you choose Switzerland instead of Monaco or Florida where a lot of the top players live?"

"I'm from here and my parents live an hour away, so I can go visit them when I'm home." Robin studied the coffee in his mug. "Plus it gives me a chance to be alone. If I stayed in those other places, I'd be invited to hang out with the other players and I couldn't say no because then I'd look like an arrogant bastard."

"Not to be a dick or anything. Don't you already have that kind of reputation?" Quinn shrugged as he took the waffle from the iron then set it on a plate. He covered it with the berries before he slid it over to Robin. "You don't have any syrup and I don't think you should have any butter."

"No butter? What's the point of waffles if I can't have butter or syrup?" Robin frowned as he stared at the food in front of him.

"Take a bite. I promise it'll taste just as good without all that stuff people usually cover them up with. I've learned to like them with fruit instead." Quinn quickly made a small one—taking more berries and melon than waffle—for himself. "Is it all right if I eat with you?"

Robin shot a confused glance at him. "Sure. I don't care. Why ask me?"

Quinn shoved his plate to the spot next to Robin then made his way around the island to sit next to Robin. "Some of my clients only saw me as the help."

"A live-in chef. Stein told me you were a chef and a life coach."

Robin took a bite of his breakfast and moaned, which brought a smile to Quinn's face.

"I'm not sure about that whole life coach thing. It wasn't something I planned on being. I didn't actually take any classes on it. I liked to cook and once I got out of rehab for my legs, I went to culinary school." He grimaced. "My second job was working as a chef for a country star. She was on the edge and barely hanging on — mentally, emotionally and physically. Her manager thought if I could get her eating right, maybe it would get her focused back on her music."

"So she could make him more money, I'm sure," Robin muttered, taking another bite.

Quinn chuckled. "You would think that, but not every manager — or agent — is out just to make money. He really cared about her and didn't want her burning out or even killing herself with all her shit. I moved into her condo, set up a diet for her to follow, and listened when she needed to talk. I taught her to meditate because there was so much junk in her head, she couldn't organize it enough to think."

"Which star?"

"I can't say. Signed a confidentiality clause when I took the job. I'm not supposed to talk about the different clients I've had. Except for DeShon Jefferson, an American football player. He was my very first client and pretty open about having me help him, and because of him, I kept getting jobs. People talked up my life coaching skills as well as my cooking chops." Quinn shrugged. "I do what I can to help people get out of their own way. God knows I was messed up after I lost my legs."

Robin took a huge bite of his waffle to give himself time to think. God, his outburst upon seeing Quinn's wheelchair had been cringeworthy. *Great impression, asshole.* He didn't know how to go back and say that it had just surprised him, especially after seeing him standing the night before. And especially how fit he'd looked. He winced. See, that wasn't really much better. It was pretty small-minded to think that just because someone was missing a couple of limbs that they couldn't be in top condition.

He knew he should respond to Quinn's summary of his skills and the little opening he'd thrown out about being messed up, but, unable to come up with anything that sounded good, he went back to Quinn's client. "DeShon Jefferson? I can't imagine what he would have needed help with. I mean, he's an All-Pro, right?" He used the last piece of waffle to clean up the rest of the fruit and shoved it all into his mouth, wondering if he could ask for another one.

Quinn looked at him curiously. "You follow American football?"

Robin swallowed as fast as he could and took a sip of coffee. "Yeah, it's a fun sport to watch…unlike baseball. That is one slow ass sport. Anyway, I got into it when I lived in the States when I was younger." He shrugged at Quinn's raised eyebrows. "Hey, I didn't always have the money or clout to choose where I wanted to live. I went to Florida to stay with Coach when I was fourteen."

Quinn's expression cleared in understanding. "Of course. That makes sense. So you probably had a tutor and so forth." At Robin's nodded confirmation, he continued, "How long have you lived here in this house?"

Robin shifted impatiently. God, were they going to talk about him all day? "I don't remember. Five years maybe? Look, not to be rude, but I'm still really hungry…"

"Say no more. I'll fix you another waffle. Did you like it with the fruit?"

That had to be a rhetorical question based on how fast Robin had wolfed it down. "Fishing for compliments?" he taunted.

It wasn't just the height advantage when Quinn stood over Robin that gave the impression he was looking down on him. "No," he returned mildly. "Just trying to find out what appeals to you. That's my job." He walked over and gave the batter a stir, his back to Robin.

Fuck. "You know what? I'm really not that hungry after all." He shoved back from the counter and stood. Damned if he was going to offer up sweet words about Quinn's food when Quinn was treating him like a long-suffering teacher would an unruly child. As though he'd already made up his mind all about Robin.

Whatever. He could care less what the guy thought of him. All he had to do was eat his damn food for three months or whatever—the rest of his life was his own. He defiantly topped off his coffee, splashed a bit too much sugar in to make a point then headed upstairs to change into workout clothes. Quinn didn't say a word to stop him as he left.

Fine with him.

Chapter Seven

Quinn glanced up from the list he'd been making as Robin strolled into the kitchen. "Taking advantage of not being at a tournament?"

"What do you mean?" Robin poured a cup of coffee without even glancing in Quinn's direction.

"Considering it's almost noon, I thought maybe you were taking a few days to rest up after the debacle that was the French Open." Quinn chose to ignore the amount of sugar Robin was pouring into his mug. Jumping on Robin right away wasn't going to get him anywhere. Hell, something had set the man off yesterday, leading Robin to spend the rest of the day avoiding him.

"Fuck you." Robin sipped on his coffee as he leaned against the counter to stare out of the backyard.

"No thanks. Who do I talk to about ordering groceries?" He went back to his list.

"I don't know. I guess it would be Margerite."

"Who's Margerite?" He didn't think that was the maid's name.

Robin shot him a quick glance. "She's the housekeeper. I would've thought Stein would've introduced you to her yesterday."

"There was only a maid here when I arrived. You'll have to ask Stein where Margerite is. I guess I can order this stuff online and have it delivered," he muttered as he tapped his pen on the paper.

"Whatever you want."

Quinn had had enough. He threw the pen down then stood. "All right. I have no idea what I did yesterday that pissed you off. Tell me what it was and I'll try never to do it again. We need to be able to talk to each other or none of this will work. I need to know that you'll listen to me when I ask you to try things and you need to believe that I know what I'm talking about. I'm not going to give you a new diet or new training techniques to mess with your mind."

Robin whirled on him. "You've already judged me as a useless bastard. Why should I do anything to help you?"

"Judged you? When did I judge you?" He admitted to himself that Robin hadn't made a good first impression and he might have started to create a profile of the man, but he hoped he'd done a better job hiding how he really felt.

"Yesterday at breakfast. I could tell you thought I was a whiny brat who needed to be disciplined for acting like a child." Robin practically spat the words at him.

"Whoa!" Quinn held up his hands to stop Robin's tirade. "Dude, I think you have mental issues that you need to work on along with your diet to get your head back in the game. At no point did I ever think you deserve to be punished for what you haven't accomplished this year."

"See? Right there." Robin slammed his mug on the counter. "That's what I'm talking about. What I haven't accomplished this year. If that's not judging, I don't know what is."

Quinn inhaled deeply. "Okay. Listen. I'm only saying what I'm pretty sure you yourself have thought. Come on, man. Are you really happy with what you've done so far? Are you happy that you went out in the first round in the French when you're one of the top seeds and tend to be the favorite every year? Think before you yell at me. You're mad at yourself, Robin, and you need to stop running from the problem."

Robin glared at him, but didn't say anything. Quinn hoped that meant the guy was thinking about what he'd said. He strolled across to the refrigerator then pulled out a chilled bottle of water. He glanced over at Robin.

"I'm going to be doing laps in the pool. You're welcome to join me and we can discuss the few changes I'd like to see in your training routine. I'm not a personal trainer, so I've already talked to your coach about it." He stopped right before he left the kitchen. "Trust me. I know how intrusive this must seem to you. I've had something like this happen to me when I had to relearn how to walk with these legs instead of the ones I was born with. It's hard having someone else in your life twenty-four hours, seven days a week. I'm here to help you, Robin."

He detoured to his room to change into his swim trunks and get into his chair. He only had one pair of legs and they weren't the right kind for swimming. It didn't matter since one of his therapy workouts had been swimming—it had helped to keep his leg muscles strong.

Rolling out to the side of the pool, he looked around to orient himself to where would be the best spot to place the chair. It was going to be difficult to get in and out of the pool. *Maybe I should ask Robin if I could get a lift installed.* He wasn't sure asking for a favor would go over well with him at the moment, though.

After ten minutes of wrangling, Quinn slid into the pool. He moaned softly as the water supported his body and his muscles were able to relax. He kicked his legs enough to keep above the surface while enjoying the buoyancy of floating.

"Is there an easier way to get in? That seems like a lot of work just to swim."

He didn't jerk, even though he hadn't known Robin had been watching him. At least he hadn't offered to help. "Yes. There's a chair lift that could be installed that I could use to get in and out of the pool."

Robin nodded. "If you send me a link, I can have Margerite organize getting one put in."

"Thanks." He must not have been able to hide his surprise.

"Hey, I'm not a complete ass. I just found out about you being hired to help me two days ago. I have the right to be a little upset. That being said, I don't want to make you struggle just because I'm pissed off. If I can help make things a little easier for you, then I will." Robin shrugged. "Can I join you?"

"Sure." Quinn watched as Robin slid into the water close by him. He ignored Robin's chiseled chest and washboard abs. *I don't lust after straight guys. Nothing I've read even hints at him liking guys.* "Your coach says that you run and lift weights as part of your training regime."

Robin agreed. "Yes—how much depends on whether I'm ramping up for a tournament or coming off one. I spend a lot of time on the court, though. Yesterday was an anomaly. Coach always makes me take a day off after coming home. So this morning I ended up over at Jerome's for a few hours of hitting and drills. I even waited until I was home again before I had coffee." Robin looked a bit smug at the end, obviously relishing revealing that instead of sleeping in, he'd been hard at work.

Quinn chose not to react to Robin's revelation. "Great. I want you to add some swimming into your routine. Instead of doing as many miles as you've been running...do a half hour of laps. It'll be easier on your knees and also more relaxing."

Robin's expression changed dramatically. "What makes you think anything's wrong with my knees?" His voice was tense.

"You had that injury last year, and trust me, no matter what the doctors say, no one ever comes back a hundred percent from a knee injury. Not even if you were eighteen and at the peak of health. To be honest, though, your knees aren't why I want you to swim." Quinn pursed his lips as he tried to think about how to explain his philosophy about swimming. "Swimming is going to become another way for you to meditate."

Robin ducked under the water then came up and ran his hands across his face and over his hair. Quinn got the impression he was stalling to think. He was starting to notice Robin's tics. Finally Robin took the bait. "Meditate, huh. That keeps coming up with you. Not sure that's really my style." He shrugged. "I mean, if it works for *you*, that's great, but I have a feeling I'd just fall asleep. And that wouldn't be very good while I'm swimming." The first hint of a smile Quinn had ever seen on Robin teased at his mouth.

"Ha-ha. The way you'll meditate while swimming is by concentrating on your breathing while falling in to the rhythm of the laps and feeling how your body cuts through the water. Trust me. It works. The other kind of meditating you'll do is to clear your mind. I think part of your problem, Robin, that you have too much clutter in your head. Too many thoughts and ideas dancing around in there that you get frustrated because you can't focus. You haven't been able to focus for quite some time, I bet." He eyed Robin.

Robin moved away from Quinn toward the deep end so he could tread water. Really, this guy should be working for Danie, not him. Of course, Danie didn't need anyone showing him how to live clean and holistically—he could be the poster boy. Maybe he'd ask Danie sometime if he meditated...if he could find some way to work it into conversation without sounding weird. On second thought, maybe not.

"Why does everyone around me always want me to be perfect?" he muttered under his breath.

The sound of water rippling came from his left, coming closer. "Who said they wanted you to be perfect? Because I sure didn't."

Aaand, in addition to everything else he does well, Quinn evidently has incredible hearing.

Robin kept treading water and spun to face Quinn, who was about six feet away. He thought back to what Quinn had said. "I guess you didn't but it sure feels like everyone's on my case lately. You, Coach, Alfred, Danie, my family, the press..." He shook his head. "I mean, I didn't get to where I am today by being a total fuck-up. I've worked my ass off practically my whole life."

And now he sounded like a whiny crybaby. Time to zip his lips. "Whatever," he sighed and dove backwards before coming up into a backstroke.

He'd never really mastered flip-turns, so he just touched the wall then reversed and pushed off to head back down the pool, ignoring Quinn, who had started swimming as well. Robin wasn't sure how long they swam and though he had no idea what Quinn had really meant about meditating, he found himself thinking about his breathing and rhythm way more than usual. Though, how long had it been since he'd done more in the pool than jump in to cool off? The long pool was practically made for laps, but it was mostly just a nice decoration off the back patio.

He hadn't planned on swimming today either—he'd already cooled down and showered after his morning session at Jerome's—but he'd noticed Quinn struggling to get into the pool. Before he knew what he was doing, he'd run upstairs past a surprised Margerite and Anke who'd been talking in the hallway, thrown on his swim shorts then hustled back downstairs, all set to help Quinn. He'd stopped himself just in time in the doorway from the living room, thinking about how he'd react in the same situation. Probably not well.

It had been very difficult to hang back and he should have just gone back inside, but he couldn't *not* watch until Quinn had finally managed to work himself into the pool. He was sweating in sympathy at that point so he'd figured he'd just go ahead and join him. Was already in his suit anyway.

He made a mental note to definitely arrange to have whatever lift thingy Quinn had mentioned installed, if only so he didn't have to ever see that struggle again.

It made him wonder what else about his house was a problem for Quinn, and if he'd bring it up if there was.

He pulled up short as a thought occurred to him. That was all well and good for the future, but how the fuck was Quinn going to get out today? Should he ask if he could help? The last thing he wanted to do was offend the guy again, but he was probably used to swimming places that were actually accessible. What if he couldn't do it? Should he wait and see or be proactive?

"I can practically hear you thinking. What's on your mind?" Quinn was treading water with one hand on the side just a few feet away from him.

Damn it. What will make me look like less of an asshole? Offering or not offering?

He thought back to the almost ill, helpless feeling he'd had while watching Quinn work his way into the water and that decided him. "Umm..." *Here goes nothing.* "Look, I don't know how to ask this, but it didn't exactly look easy for you to get into the pool, at least from my viewpoint—and I promise I'll do something about that asap. But, uh, that was working with gravity and you're in here now and so I was just wondering..."

To his surprise, Quinn smiled. "It will actually be easier for me to get up into the chair than you might think." He turned so he was fully facing Robin, his back to the side, then braced his hands like he was doing a triceps dip. With a big heave that looked to take little effort at all, he was up and sitting on the edge.

"From here I can get myself up into the chair, though I'll wait and dry out a bit. That's one of the first things you learn in my situation—to get from the floor into the chair. It's lowering yourself out without tipping the chair or landing hard that's tough. Especially onto concrete…"

Robin barely heard Quinn's explanation. His mouth had gone dry at the offhand demonstration of Quinn's strength. The sudden jolt of attraction caught Robin off guard. With the glistening muscle definition on display, his hair and eyelashes wet and the little smirk on his face, Quinn all of a sudden hit about ten of Robin's buttons.

Oh. My. God.

The cool water was only partially successful in keeping the instant flow of blood to his cock from getting embarrassing. Time to get the hell out of here. Obviously lack of blood sugar was affecting his brain or something. No way should he be seeing his live-in chef that way. Easygoing he may be, but obviously he was a macho guy—probably ex-military from what he'd pieced together. The last thing Robin needed was to offend him with an inappropriate look.

Speaking of which…

He averted his face. "Good. Looks like you have it under control then. I'm going to…" He'd been about to say he was gonna grab something to eat, but that would sound weird to his chef. "I'm going to dry off and then maybe you and me and Margerite can sit down and"—he waved his hand as he moved toward the steps without looking at Quinn—"figure stuff out."

"That sounds great. I'll get dressed and make some lunch for you while we talk, if that's okay."

"Yes, great. See you then." He sounded like an idiot but didn't slow his escape. He snagged a towel and wrapped it tight around his waist.

Apparently strength and competence were his kryptonite.

It's going to be a long three months.

Chapter Eight

Quinn hummed softly to himself as he began to cut up the vegetables for the salads he was making for lunch. Robin had gone out to the court for a training session with his coach while Quinn had gone to the kitchen. While he got into the rhythm of cooking, he thought about the last three weeks.

They'd fallen into a rather amicable partnership after their rough start. It had taken a few days to convince Robin that the diet Quinn had put him on was the best thing for him, and Quinn had heard a lot of complaining about the stuff Robin wasn't supposed to be eating or drinking any more. Hell, Robin still got in a few digs every day about it, but Quinn had heard worse from other clients.

He frowned when he thought about the drinking aspect of Robin's nutrition. He had a sneaky feeling that Robin still drank, even after telling Quinn he'd quit. He'd never caught him with alcohol or even smelling like it. Yet the dependence Robin seemed to have on it wouldn't be easy to break.

There was nothing he could do about it until he actually caught the guy red-handed with a bottle and a drink in his hand. He had to trust that Robin really was trying to make the best of their situation and wouldn't do anything to sabotage it.

"Damaris, where the hell are you?"

He glanced up to watch Robin's coach stalk into the kitchen with a very unhappy Robin trailing behind him. "I'm right here where I'm supposed to be." He gestured in a vague circle at the area around him.

"Did you tell Robin that he was ready to play at Wimbledon?" Ramsey glared at him while crossing his arms over his chest.

"Umm…" Quinn wasn't sure what to say because he didn't want to get caught in the middle of the brewing argument. "Did he say I did?"

Robin gave him a narrow-eyed stare and Ramsey snorted.

"No, I didn't say you did. Why the hell would I need his permission to play in a tournament?" Robin demanded of his coach.

Ramsey shook his head. "You don't, but as your personal life coach and trainer, he has a say in whether you're ready to play or not. So is he?"

When both pairs of eyes pinned him where he stood, Quinn took a deep breath, set the knife down then propped his hands on his hips. "Do you want my opinion?"

"Yes."

"No."

Robin's negative statement came right on the heels of his coach's affirmative one. Quinn heaved a mental sigh. *Why do I always get caught in the middle of these situations? Why can't I ever just be the fucking chef everyone chooses to ignore except when it's time to eat?*

"Yes, we want your opinion, Damaris. You're the one who has been with him every day for the past three weeks. You're the one who has seen how much effort he's put into adopting this new routine of yours." Ramsey shrugged. "I've only seen him during his training sessions. He's getting better, more focused and maybe a little more stamina, but I don't think he's ready to play a major tournament like Wimbledon."

Quinn tugged on his bottom lip while he thought for a moment then said, "You're right. He is getting better at focusing and not letting mistakes frustrate him. We've been working on his stamina and his overall health has gotten better because of the specialized diet I put together for him."

"And he's right here in the fucking room with both you bastards," Robin practically shouted.

"But you still have a ways to go, Robin." Quinn met Robin's gaze. "I'm sorry. I don't think you're ready to play a Grand Slam event. If it was a smaller, less important tournament, I'd say go ahead. It would give you a chance to put into practice some of those calming techniques I've been teaching you. Wimbledon is too big a stage to be tweaking and working on your game. I think you should play a smaller tournament then focus on the US Open."

He thought he saw hurt flash in Robin's eyes before the anger welled in them.

"Need I remind both of you that you work for me?" Robin clenched his hands. "I get final say in where I play and I'm going to Wimbledon. I haven't missed a Grand Slam tournament for the last three years, not even when I was injured. I'm not going to start now."

Quinn and Ramsey watched as Robin stalked from the room.

"That went well," Ramsey muttered.

"Did you really think it would when you treated him like he was a child?" Quinn started filling two bowls with spinach and kale. "Then instead of sitting him down and talking to him about why you think him playing in this tournament is a bad idea, you come and ask me my advice, making it seem like you value my opinion more than anything he has to say. Man, he might be having the worse year of his pro career and be all kinds of screwed up, but he still has his pride and doesn't deserve to be treated that way."

Ramsey rubbed his chin as he stared out of the window. "I guess you're right. I hate knowing that he's not going to get any better results than he did in the French. His head isn't in the game right now and he can't play a Grand Slam even a little distracted."

Quinn threw all the different vegetables he'd cut up in the bowls before whipping up a light citrus vinaigrette dressing that he drizzled over the salads. After getting out two forks, he added all of the items to a tray. He placed a carafe of water and two glasses on it as well then shoved it in the coach's direction.

"I suggest you go find Robin, make sure he hasn't started drinking, and have lunch. Talk over strategy for the tournament because I guarantee he's going. Nothing you say or do will change his mind."

"Drinking?" Ramsey froze after grabbing the tray from the counter. "Is that something I should be worried about?"

Shaking his head, Quinn said, "No. It's something we're working on."

"You seriously need to tell me if there is. And by the way, you'll be going to England with him. Might as well start packing." Ramsey dropped that bombshell right before he left the kitchen.

"What the fuck?" Quinn got his own lunch ready then wandered back to the little patio beyond the weight room. He dropped onto one of the chairs, stretching out his legs and enjoying the easing of the weight off his prosthetics. "He can't be fucking serious. Why the hell would I go to Wimbledon with him? I'm a glorified chef, not a member of his entourage. It's not like he couldn't find someone there to cook his meals."

He ate quickly, not enjoying the salad like he normally did. *Why does traveling with Robin worry me so much? I've traveled with a lot of my clients during my career. It wouldn't be the first time.* Yet he couldn't deny that it would be the first time he'd been attracted to one of his clients before. Oh, he'd admired DeShon Jefferson and thought the football player was a stud, but it hadn't been anything more than that.

In the three weeks he and Robin had spent together, Quinn had found himself admiring the man's body way more than he should've. He'd noticed how graceful Robin's movements were — running, swimming, playing tennis — it didn't matter. Robin was one of those rare creatures — a natural athlete. Robin's confidence in his body's ability to do whatever he asked of it was a huge turn-on for Quinn, whose own body let him down almost daily.

He shook his head. No, he wasn't going down that slippery slope leading to depression and anger. He wouldn't allow himself to be jealous of Robin. Quinn had overcome a terrible accident and while his life had changed, it hadn't ended and he constantly needed to remember that.

"Back to the problem at hand." He stared at the rippling pool water. "I don't usually lust after straight guys, yet I jerk off every night thinking about Robin. If

I have to spend even more time with him than I do now, I just might end up doing something crazy like kissing him. Not good when the dude doesn't like guys."

Closing his eyes, Quinn leaned his head back, soaking up the warmth of the sun. He could protest all he wanted, but he knew the score. If Ramsey and Stein wanted him to go with Robin, then he'd go. He would control his desire and hope he didn't do something stupid that would get him fired.

"You can deal with it," Quinn told himself as he pushed to his feet. "It's not like he's going to want you hanging around him all the time anyway. He'll want to do stuff with his friends and shit like that. Just think of him as another client. There's nothing unique about him."

And if he believed that, Quinn was pretty sure someone somewhere had a bridge for him to buy.

* * * *

Robin was still fuming after Coach finally left. He'd gotten his way—he was finally going to be playing again and not missing Wimbledon—but hell, could they have treated him more like a fucking kid? He was used to it from Coach, but Quinn saying that he didn't think Robin was ready to play a tournament he'd been playing in since he was a teenager? After he'd thought they'd become sort of friends? That hurt.

He's not your friend—he's an employee. And not even your employee so you can't fire him.

You know you're just embarrassed because he's hot and you want to impress him.

"Gah!" He ran his hands through his hair and gave it a hard yank. His cell phone chimed with a text. He picked it up, anxious for a distraction from his mood. The text was from Jerome.

Popping over in a few. Have a present for you.

Thank God. Talk about perfect timing. He'd run out of Soma a few days ago and had been edgy ever since. His knee had been fine, but it made him nervous to not have any on hand. Just in case.

He lingered up in his suite, not wanting to face Quinn just yet. The doorbell finally rang, and by the time Robin got downstairs, Jerome was already waiting in the entry. But instead of Margerite, Quinn was standing there talking to him. *Shit.*

"Since when do you answer the door?" He immediately regretted his fear-driven question. *Way to play it cool, Keller.*

Jerome couldn't hide a smile, while Quinn frowned at Robin. "Since I knew you were upstairs and Margerite went to run some errands. Problem?"

"No, not at all," he backtracked. "Just...don't want you to feel like an employee or anything."

"But isn't that exactly what he is, when you come right down to it?" Jerome said in German to Robin.

Robin squinted at him, not sure he liked the designation or the haughty tone. He hoped Quinn didn't speak the language. "Be nice, asshole. He's more than an employee," he returned in kind. Switching to English to be polite, he added, "Come on in. Would you like a drink? We could sit out on the patio."

"I can't stay." Jerome shook his head. "I just wanted to see if you still have my lucky shirt. I think I remember you borrowing it that one time."

Lucky shirt? Robin couldn't keep his eyebrows from going up. "Okaaay. Hell if I know." He finally twigged to what Jerome was getting at. *Oh...privacy, duh.* "Come up to my room and you can take a look for it if you want."

"Great. You know I can't go to Wimbledon without it." Jerome headed toward the living room. "Did you get everything all straightened out with Ramsey? He's not still being a prick and trying to tell you you can't go, is he? I'd so fire him if he ever tried that with me."

Robin glanced uncomfortably at Quinn, who looked less than impressed, then he followed Jerome up the stairs. "He's not being a prick. He just doesn't want my first tournament back after the French to be such a circus, like it always is at the Grand Slams. But yeah, I'm still going." As soon as they were in the upstairs hallway, he whispered, "Lucky shirt? Really?"

Jerome laughed. "Hey, it was the best I could come up with. That guy looked like he was going to stand there all day watching every little thing. You didn't want me handing these over to you right in front of him, did you?" He put his hand in his front pocket and pulled out the muscle relaxant bottle that Robin knew had one of Jerome's employee's sister's name on it. He gave it a little shake.

"Fuck no. Give me that." He snatched it out of Jerome's hand and propelled him into his room with a little shove for good measure. "Go 'look for your shirt', since it would look really stupid if we walked right back downstairs." He closed the door then crossed the room to his bookshelf and tucked the Soma safely behind a copy of Lance Armstrong's *It's Not About the Bike*.

Of course Robin would never take steroids or anything else—he just liked the irony. He'd actually had a prescription for Soma at one point, and he always transferred the pills to an old bottle with his name on it that he'd kept. Plausible deniability if it ever popped up during a drug test. He tried not to let his elaborate machinations bother him. It wasn't like he was addicted or anything.

"Relax. If anything, he probably thinks I'm a booty call." Jerome threw himself down on Robin's bed, grinning at him and waggling his eyebrows like an idiot. "How long do you think it usually takes you to get off?" He lay on his back and humped the air.

"Ugh. I never want to see you do that again. And you're not my type. You're straight and you're an asshole."

Jerome was one of the few people who knew Robin was gay and he never failed to get his digs in. With all the teasing, sometimes he would have wondered about Jerome's orientation, except he knew what a player Jerome was. If there was a hint of anything besides strictly hetero leanings to him, he would definitely have made the moves on Robin by now.

"Hey, nobody's perfect. So, all kidding aside, I'm glad you're going to Wimbledon, Robin. It wouldn't have been the same without you." Since they were hitting partners and both were coached by Ramsey, they usually traveled to tournaments together, though they seldom played against one another. Jerome was a solid player, but he had never broken the top fifty in singles and hadn't made the draw for either the French or Wimbledon this year. However, he was half of one of the best mixed doubles teams playing right now, which is what he'd be focused on when he wasn't helping Robin with his workouts.

"Thanks."

Jerome might be a spoiled brat and had the social skills of a teenager, but he really was a good friend. Robin walked over to his dresser and began sorting through T-shirts. Toward the bottom of the drawer, he stopped and pulled one out.

"Here you go. Your new lucky shirt." He tossed it onto the bed.

Jerome picked it up and held it up. "Really?" Below the yellow smiley face was printed '*Have a nice day*'.

"Hey, that's a classic. Totally lucky shirt material. Can't wait to see you wearing it at Wimbledon after you made such a big deal about it." He winked then laughed and ducked as Jerome threw the balled up shirt at his head.

Chapter Nine

"Fucking rain delays," Robin mumbled. What was it about Wimbledon? Tradition, shmdition—someone should seriously think about moving the tournament to a less rainy month. In all the years he'd been coming here, there was maybe only one where he hadn't had at least one lengthy delay, if not several.

His first round match had been suspended due to the weather, so he and the other player were waiting around to see if they would get to resume play anytime soon. Robin was currently up two sets, even at two in the third. Even if he went back on the court and finished strong, they had at least a half hour left to wrap up that match, and it could be hours if his opponent made a good run at him.

He blew out a sharp exhalation and changed his playlist again, unable to settle on any music that worked, wishing he could go hit with someone. With the delay he'd had way too much time to think about how the match had gone so far, the first one in competition since he'd lost so badly at Roland Garros a month ago. Thank God he had the first two sets in the bank.

The door opened and an official came in. Robin removed his headphones and braced himself for the news.

"The radar is showing it clearing off, so we plan to resume play in twenty minutes," she told them.

"Thank God," he muttered. He raised his hand in acknowledgment and stood, adrenaline already starting to pump him up. He got started on his pre-match routine right away—twenty minutes wasn't very long at all.

Let's put this one away, Keller.

* * * *

He was repeating the same thing to himself an hour later. Neither of them had broken serve, so the third set had gone to a tiebreak. He just had to win on his serve, break once and he'd win the match.

Come on. Let's put this one away.

His first serve from the deuce court grazed the net. "Let! First service," the chair umpire announced.

Robin took a long breath, blew it out then tossed the ball and reared back to put his all into the serve. It was a deep, wide serve and took Kroener off the court. His backhand went into the net. *Yes!*

"One—love, Keller."

God, he could almost taste it. He got into position to receive serve and threw all of Kroener's momentum right back at him, catching him in no-man's-land coming in to the net. He managed to get a racquet on it, but couldn't get it over the net.

"Two—love, Keller."

The next serve was a good one and Kroener took the point after Robin's weak return got pounded back down the sideline for a win. Robin followed up by holding serve easily to put him up at four — one.

It felt so damn good to be focused and having things go his way. Did he have Quinn to thank? Hard to tell, but something in his life was working.

Kroener's first serve was a bit off-speed but Robin adjusted and put it in play near the baseline. It was one of the longer points of the set, but he finally caught Kroener going the wrong way and painted the line.

Two more points.

Keep your cool, Keller. You can't celebrate until it's over.

Then Kroener double-faulted.

"Double match point, Keller."

Robin fought to stay focused. He took his time accepting the balls from the ball boy then tucked one in his pocket. The sun peeked out just as he approached the service line. A deep breath later he was rocking into his serve. And aced it.

"Game, set, match, Keller."

Robin went to his knees as the roar went up from the Court One crowd. After a moment, he hopped back up and pounded the ball from his pocket deep into the stands. Then he jogged to the net to shake hands with Kroener. After doing the same with the chair umpire, he took a moment to walk back out onto the court and wave in each direction, clapping to thank them for their applause.

He noticed the usher moving in and finally went to gather his stuff together, feeling a bit guilty for his celebration when they probably wanted to get the next two players onto the court to warm up. It was only a first round win, but God, it had felt good to break that onus.

After taking part in the usual post-match interviews, he finally got to clean up and dress in his street clothes. Stein wasn't here, and Coach had left a message that he planned to make his way over to one of the outer courts to watch the end of the match determining his next opponent. He never looked up at the player's boxes while he was on the court, but he knew Quinn had come to watch the match. They'd gotten him credentials for similar access as Ramsey would have, which made it easier for him to move about the grounds.

Robin was on his way through the empty slanted hallway under Court One to meet up with Quinn just outside the private entrance for players and staff when he heard his name called in a low, familiar voice. "Robin."

A moment later, Danie yanked Robin up against him and bent down to whisper, "Missed you, Robbie," before kissing him silly. Frozen with shock at first, he quickly melted. How he'd ever thought Danie wasn't into kissing he had no idea. He lost his head at that point, still buzzing from his victory, and had acquiesced to the wordless demands as Danie pinned him against the wall and ravaged his mouth and neck. Hands under his ass urged him to wrap his legs around Danie's hips, and they rutted against one another.

"Someone might come along. I know a place," Danie finally said when they came up for air. The words were like a shock of cold water and had him ready to grab his bag and get the hell out of there before they were seen.

Instead, he followed Danie as he led him to some sort of utility closet. Once inside, he put a hand up against Danie's chest when he leaned back in.

"What's this all about? Since when are you so happy to see me that you'd risk exposure?" *And kiss me?*

"Just as I said, *brah*. Missed you this past month." Danie's accent was thick as could be as he ran his hand down over Robin's hard-as-nails cock, the layers of cloth doing nothing but making Robin wish they were gone. "Feels like you missed me too."

"Fuck."

"I wish. This'll have to do." Danie quickly undid the zip of Robin's khakis then followed suit with his own pants. Taking both their cocks into his grip, he bent to rest his mouth against the hollow of Robin's neck and shoulder while he stroked. He paused and licked his palm then resumed the hard rhythm, definitely designed to get them off quickly.

Robin groaned then sucked his lips in and bit hard, trying to keep quiet as his orgasm hit like a ton of bricks. Danie spun him away just in time to keep from making a mess of their clothes, giving Robin his other palm to thrust along while he came, cupping it to catch most of his cum.

He was almost dizzy with pleasure but had the presence of mind to reach and encircle Danie's thick cock behind Danie's grip. "Let me," he whispered. Danie let go then switched to grasp his own cock with his wet hand, coating it with Robin's cum.

It didn't take long for Robin to have Danie bucking into his hand, catching his own release just like before. The sound of their heavy breathing filled the small space for a minute while they recovered, then Robin looked down and fought a chuckle.

"What are you going to do with that? Should've just let it hit the floor."

"God, you're a heathen." Danie looked around. "Where's your bag?"

Robin stilled. "Shit, I left it in the hallway."

Danie blew out a frustrated breath then began wiping his hand on his own shirt. Robin's mouth dropped open.

"I can't believe you just did that. You, of all people."

"Didn't have much choice, now did I? At least I layered." When his hand was dry, he carefully pulled his shirt up over his head, revealing a gray performance tee underneath—with his sponsor's logo, of course.

Robin tucked himself away and zipped up...and quickly found himself with a hand full of Danie's shirt.

"Here you go. You can take it home and wash it for me." Danie also put his pants to rights.

Robin stared at the shirt then up at Danie. "What the hell? Me? Why me?"

"Because you have a bag you can tuck it into, unlike me. And I like that shirt—don't want to throw it away. My luck some fan would see it and pull it out of the trash. And that would be just..." Danie gave a shudder that Robin echoed.

"Okay, yeah, that does not need to happen. Fine. I'll take it."

Danie slowly opened the door then after a survey of the tunnel, stepped out. Robin followed him and hustled over to where his bag thankfully still sat.

"Heard you have someone staying at your place with you this time around," Danie said while he was bent to put the shirt into his bag. The words sounded casual but hit Robin like a shot to the solar plexus.

Was that what this was all about? Was Danie...jealous?

He zipped the compartment shut then straightened slowly. "Yes—Quinn. He's..." Robin wondered why he felt compelled to explain the situation. "He's my new personal chef and team member. After the French...well, they decided I needed to try something new."

"Ah." That was all Danie said and Robin couldn't tell by his tone what he was thinking. "You played well today. Whatever he's doing, it must be working."

There was the sound of footsteps a few seconds before a group of four people appeared at the upper end of the tunnel. They moved closer to the wall to let the group go by. As they passed they murmured congratulations to Robin and cast admiring glances at Danie. Here, everyone knew who they were.

Robin was stupidly glad they hadn't come by about five minutes sooner. Danie had taken an insane chance today—and for what? Robin still didn't know, exactly. Was it simply that he was pent up, that Danie hadn't been with anyone since Paris? Had Robin's victory made him want to celebrate with Robin? Or was Danie jealous of Quinn's presence? That would mean that he had feelings for Robin that he'd never in a million years suspected were there.

An odd, niggling sensation burrowed deep into his chest at the thought of Quinn. It was almost like...guilt, or perhaps regret. The funny thing was, he didn't have anything to feel guilty about. And why would he feel anything like regret for finally getting closer to Danie, something he'd wanted for such a long time and had thought to be an impossible dream?

Chapter Ten

Staying in the shadows, Quinn had been relieved to see Robin walking down the hall toward him. He technically wasn't supposed to be in this hallway, but security had seen his badge and offered to let him wait inside since it had started raining again. He had been about to call out when he'd spotted another man approaching Robin. Quinn had barely swallowed his gasp as he'd watched the stranger put his arms around Robin's waist, tug him close then bend down to kiss him.

Holy shit! My gaydar has been completely off about him.

He'd been stunned when Robin had glanced around then dropped his bag to encircle the guy's neck. Whoever he was had Robin pinned against the wall and lifted him enough for Robin to wrap his legs around him. It hadn't been until Quinn had heard Robin moan that he snapped out of his shock enough to feel embarrassed at watching the men together.

"Someone might come along. I know a place..." The accent wasn't familiar but there had been no mistaking the tall guy's implication as he'd set Robin down then led him back up the hall. Slowly walking away until he could turn without them seeing or hearing him, Quinn had made his way outside then across the grounds to where the taxis were parked, all the while thinking about what he'd just witnessed.

He wasn't about to wait around for Robin now. No way to know how long it would take for him to get done with his quickie. Quinn slid into the backseat of the cab, giving the driver the address of their townhouse.

He closed his eyes then immediately opened them, not wanting to replay the scene he'd just left. His cock was hard and he adjusted himself in his pants. All those sexy noises Robin had made while the guy kissed him had got Quinn all hot and bothered, but he was still a little in shock over the fact that he hadn't figured out Robin was into men.

Why had he been so willing to overlook the possibility? Had he been worried that if he thought there might have been a hint of interest on Robin's part, Quinn might have done something to get the man into his bed? He'd never been promiscuous, though he'd had probably more than his fair share of lovers — before and after the accident.

He wasn't sure about mixing business with pleasure. Robin was a client, and Quinn had certain responsibilities that sleeping with Robin might confuse. They had a lot more work to do, but he believed he could help Robin get back to the top of his sport. Sleeping with Robin wouldn't do anything except harm.

Why am I even thinking about this? He's never made one move to make me think he's interested. He probably doesn't want a cripple for a lover. He winced at the negative voice in his head. A voice he hadn't heard in quite some time and one he'd hoped he'd banished forever.

Once the taxi got him to the townhouse, he paid the driver then made his way slowly up the steps to the door. Standing there, he stared at it for a moment before unlocking it. He walked in then made his way to the back of the house where his suite was located.

He sighed in relief at the sight of his chair. His stumps ached from him climbing up and down stairs at Center Court where Robin had played his first match. All Quinn wanted to do was go take a shower, change into some sweats and a T-shirt then sit for a while.

He'd put some chicken in the refrigerator to marinate for their dinner, but he wasn't entirely sure Robin would be coming home to eat. He was probably going somewhere with the mystery man. Quinn rubbed his suddenly tight chest at the thought.

Enough already. Get your act together. If he isn't home when you get out of the bath, text to find out if he's coming. Don't be a baby about it.

After removing his prosthetics, Quinn settled in his chair then rolled himself into his bathroom to take a shower. There had been a time when he'd never have lingered, liking the idea of a quick in-and-out shower, but once his legs had been removed, he found soaking in warm water for a while helped ease his muscles and the soreness of his stumps.

He settled onto the bench in the shower stall then leaned his head back against the tiles. Closing his eyes, he thought about how surprised Ramsey and Stein had been when Robin had won his first match. Quinn could've told them it would happen. Robin was out to prove them all wrong and it was that determination that had got him through the first round.

Unfortunately, Quinn didn't think that emotion was going to get Robin much further.

He should start thinking about how to help Robin deal with his disappointment when that loss happened. There were things Robin needed to learn from the experience, yet all Quinn could think about was that fucking kiss. He slid his hand down over his stomach to wrap his fingers around his shaft. As he began to stroke, he tightened his grip, imagining he was fucking Robin's firm ass. Robin would be whimpering and begging him to fuck him harder and faster.

Quinn had been primed to come from the moment he fled from the scene of the kiss. So it didn't take him long, just a few good strong pulls and he climaxed, moaning loudly. He managed to keep from slipping to the floor of the shower by catching himself with his hands on the edge of the bench. When he finally could think clearly again, he soaped up then rinsed off.

He was climbing into his chair before going back into his bedroom to dress when he heard Robin calling his name. He tugged on some briefs then pushed himself toward the door. Before he got there, it swung open.

Robin walked in. "There you are. I thought you were going to wait for me."

"I was. I mean, I wanted to, but my legs were really bothering me. I guess I wasn't quite ready for all the walking and stairs today." He tried not to stare at Robin's kiss-swollen lips or the little red bite mark barely visible by his collar. "I just wanted to get back here and take them off. I'm sorry I forgot about texting you to let you know."

He moved toward the bed where he'd laid out his sweats and T-shirt. Robin didn't seem in any hurry to leave the room, so Quinn took the towel off then tossed it on the cover, reaching for his sweats.

"Congratulations on your win. You looked pretty good out there," he commented while sitting with his back to Robin. He hated having people watch him dress. There were still times when he struggled to get pants on for some reason and he disliked the thought of people pitying him for not being able to get dressed as quickly as a more able-bodied person did.

"Thanks. I'm stoked, man." Robin seemed to be on edge and Quinn couldn't help but wonder if all that excitement was from the win or if some of it had to do with the make-out scene afterwards.

"Why don't you go get comfortable and I'll get dinner started?" he suggested after tugging his shirt on. He shoved his hair off his forehead then turned to face Robin. "I have some chicken and steamed veggies for us."

"Cool. I'll be back in a few." Robin dashed out of the room and Quinn smiled.

He turned on the small, under-cabinet TV when he got the kitchen. As he started the chicken cooking and got the vegetables prepped, he watched the recap of the day's events at Wimbledon, enjoying the effusive reporting on Robbie's win and how he'd played.

"In other news, top seeded Danie Coetzee has been seen on the grounds at the All England Club, even though he has a first round bye and won't be playing until day three of the tournament..."

Quinn felt his mouth drop open when he stared at the picture of the man whom he'd seen kiss Robin a short time earlier.

Holy Mother of God. Robin's lover is Danie Coetzee, one of the top tennis players in the world.

Chapter Eleven

Robin's mind was spinning and he was on an extreme high that had nothing to do with stimulants. Between the relief at his win, being accosted by Danie in the tunnel then being treated to the sight of Quinn fresh out of the shower, Robin's good karma seemed to be in overdrive today.

He caught a glimpse of himself in the dresser mirror while he was getting some sweatpants out of a drawer. Lightly touching the faint hickey, then his lips, Robin shook his head. He still had no idea what had gotten into Danie today. "Crazy Afrikaner."

Wondering if Quinn would notice or be able to tell what the red mark was, Robin undressed then decided to take a shower of his own, if only to rinse the reminder of his encounter from his skin before he had dinner with Quinn. That made him recall how Quinn had looked, damp from the shower and wearing only some briefs. It was embarrassing how excited he'd been to see Quinn—the guy was probably wondering if he had any sense of personal boundaries, following him around like a puppy. But he'd missed him at their meeting place. He'd really been looking forward to seeing him right after the win, celebrating with him while still high from the match. Instead, he'd done his celebrating with Danie.

The tight sensation from before returned and he began to get irritated with himself. Danie was Danie — he'd been an intimate part of Robin's life for a long time. Quinn was a temporary feature…and a paid one at that.

Reminding himself of their respective places didn't do much to sort out the confusing jumble of images in Robin's head as he soaped his semi-erect cock and balls. Danie's kisses mingled with Quinn's muscular chest and arms. Suddenly he had a full hard-on.

Hell.

Knowing he had sweatpants waiting for him, he was going to have to choose. Get off? Or go with a cold shower? A quick turn of the faucet and couple of minutes later he was more happy to get out, dry off and put on warm, soft clothes knowing he wasn't going to embarrass himself when he went down for dinner.

Once he was in his around-the-house clothes, he headed back downstairs. Quinn was dressed similarly to him and was still sautéing the chicken breasts.

"What can I do to help?" he offered.

"Can you get a couple of plates? I made a pitcher of iced green tea, too, if you'd like some with dinner."

The TV caught his attention — they were showing the current brackets. It gave him a small burst of pride to see his name as having advanced, then he rolled his eyes at himself. *Pretty lame to be so excited about getting out of the first round.* "Mind if I shut this off?"

"Go ahead. I was just keeping up on what's going on in the tournament while I cooked."

Robin clicked it off then helped Quinn get their places set with the simple meal. "One more thing." He wheeled back over to the small oven, put on a mitt and opened it.

"Oh my God. Really?" The warm bread smelled amazing as Quinn pulled it out. Robin was almost drooling. He hardly got any sort of bread anymore.

"It's whole grain with spelt." Quinn closed the oven then brought the bread over to the table, wheeling with one hand while carrying the hot, foil-wrapped loaf with the mitt.

"Whatever. It's bread. Can I have butter too?"

"Try it without first."

Robin grumbled. "Fine."

It turned out he didn't need any butter at all. He put away three thick slices of the bread before Quinn cut him off, claiming he would go into a carb coma if he ate any more.

"Not hardly, though I might get a belly." He ran his hand over his abs, knowing full well that was something he wouldn't have to worry about for a very long time, if ever.

"Wouldn't want that to happen. Guys like guys with six-packs." Quinn popped the last bite of his own piece of bread into his mouth.

It took a moment for what Quinn had said to register, but when it did, Robin froze.

Guys like guys…

Oh God, he knows.

Quinn saw the utter panic in Robin's eyes and he couldn't allow the man to worry anymore about what Quinn was thinking. He tapped the back of Robin's fist to get his attention. When he met his gaze, Quinn smiled.

"Don't worry, man. I'm not interested in telling anyone your secrets. I'm here for you, not for what I gain."

"You signed a nondisclosure agreement," Robin pointed out.

Chuckling, Quinn nodded. "You're right. I did, but even without that, I wouldn't blab to the press about you. What happens in your house stays between us." He stopped then qualified. "Stays between you, Ramsey, Stein and me. Though I don't think that you liking guys needs to be their business either. Unless they know."

Robin swallowed then nodded. "Thanks. There aren't many people who know about me."

"I have to admit, you've done a great job at hiding it. When I researched you before heading to Switzerland, I never got a hint that you might be gay." Quinn went back to eating, trying to calm his heartbeat. It was obvious that Robin belonged to Danie, and Quinn would bet it was a long-standing affair. He didn't have a chance, plus he wasn't about to move in on another guy's territory.

"How did you find out?"

He didn't want to admit he'd been spying on Robin and Danie in the hallway under Court One, but he couldn't just say he'd figured it out since it wasn't the truth. He'd had no clue about Robin's leanings, which shouldn't surprise him. They'd only been together for four weeks and there hadn't been a lot of visitors while in Switzerland to see how Robin acted around people.

"I was waiting for you in the hallway under Court One. I saw Danie approach you, though I didn't know who he was until I saw his picture on TV." Quinn winked at Robin. "I don't follow tennis, so I'm not up on who the big name players are and what they look like."

"God, he's going to freak," Robin muttered.

"Don't worry. Hell, you don't even have to tell him I know if you don't want to. It's not like I'm going to run up to him and tell him I saw you two."

Why am I doing all this just to reassure him I won't say a word? I guess if he believes me about this, he'll trust me more about other things. He wasn't sure that was his real reason or not, but it was the only one he was willing to admit to at the moment.

"Thanks." Robin seemed to relax slightly. "I'm glad you're okay with it."

"Okay with it? Why wouldn't I be? I'm gay too," he announced, and Robin shot him a quick glance.

"You are? But you never said anything." Before Quinn could reply to that, Robin held up his hand. "I know. That was stupid to say. It's not something one tends to discuss with a person they've just met and we don't really talk about our personal lives, do we?"

Shrugging, Quinn agreed. "We don't, and to be honest, we probably should talk a little more. There's nothing exciting about my life, but I have a feeling that part of your inability to focus during your matches is because you have so much other shit going on in your head. I'm not saying it's good or bad. It just is, and we have to figure out how to get you to concentrate on the games until you're done with the matches."

Robin started to push his plate away and Quinn shook his head. "No. You have to eat all of that. I know you have a day off tomorrow then you play your second round match the next day. Ramsey called to tell me that he wants you at the club by nine in the morning to get some hitting in."

"Why didn't he text me?"

"Have you checked your phone? More than likely he did. He also lets me know your schedule so I have a clue what's going on. As long as I travel with you, he'll include me."

"Do you have a boyfriend back in America?" Robin blurted out the question then flushed. "Or is that too personal a question to ask?"

Quinn grinned. "I'm pretty sure that if I get to dig into your personal life, I have to be willing to answer questions about mine. It's only fair right?"

Nodding, Robin stuffed a piece of the chicken in his mouth and moaned. Quinn loved how much Robin seemed to enjoy the meals he cooked for him. Even when he wasn't a hundred percent sure about how they would taste, Robin still tried them and more often than not, ended up clearing his entire plate. After being with the man for a few weeks, Quinn had figured out that while Robin ate rather healthy foods, he didn't eat enough calories to make up for all the ones he burned. Doing that could actually slow a person's metabolism down and cause them other health problems. He would've thought that Ramsey would have had a nutritionist talk to Robin about that part of his training, but either he hadn't or Robin hadn't listened.

"I've had a few serious relationships, if you want to call them that. They only lasted a few months each. Not one of them ever got to the point where we were thinking about committing our lives to each other. Since I lost my legs eight years ago, there hasn't even really been dating. I've hooked up with a few guys when it got bad, but I've been too busy getting my life back in order to be concerned about a personal life."

"Who's the guy you talk to and email all the time?" Robin raised one eyebrow at Quinn's inquiring gaze. "I wasn't eavesdropping or anything. I just happened to walk by that patio a few times when you've been talking to him."

Quinn pushed his empty plate away from him as he leaned back in his chair. "That's Morgan, my older brother. He works for the government doing God knows what. I've never gotten up the nerve to ask for details. As long as he comes back from his jobs, I'm happy. He's always been overprotective, so he makes me call him once a week and email as often as I can."

"Must be nice," Robin muttered.

"I take it you don't have any brothers or sisters," Quinn said, rolling away from the table to the counter where he'd set the container of homemade granola. He'd baked it yesterday while Robin was at the club practicing. "Take a handful. It'll be dessert for tonight."

"Thanks. And no siblings." Robin went quiet but Quinn sensed he had more to say, so he waited him out. "My parents are technically my aunt and uncle, but they've raised me since I was a toddler. I don't remember my mother. I used to, or maybe I just thought I did, but all I can picture when I think of her now are photos. After she died, Mom and Da took me in. They'd never been able to have children and Mom was about fifteen years older than my mother." He rolled his shoulders uncomfortably. "Anyway, they're getting older and traveling is hard on them, so if I didn't live where I do, I'd never see them."

Quinn didn't mention that in the time he'd been with Robin, he only knew of two times that he'd gone to see them. "What about your father?"

"Never knew who he was," Robin admitted quietly.

"Ah." No wonder there was a pervasive sense of loneliness surrounding Robin. The lack of family plus all the years living away from a normal environment, all the traveling. No school chums or neighbors. It explained a lot. "Well, don't be too jealous about Morgan. Having an older brother isn't all it's cracked up to be at times, but I wouldn't want to know what it was like to live without him."

"While I'm at the US Open, maybe he could come to New York to see you. I'd like to meet him." Robin popped a few clusters of granola into his mouth then tilted his head as he chewed. "Mmm. I like this. Anyway, does Morgan know? That you're gay, I mean."

"Oh yeah. He figured it out a long time ago without me even saying anything to him. He showed up at my place one day and asked when I was going to introduce him to my boyfriend. I just laughed, but I thought my boyfriend was going to shit himself." Quinn smiled at the memory. "At the time, Morgan had just returned from an overseas job. He had a full beard, long hair, and looked like he hadn't bathed in weeks. He also had this slightly wild-eyed expression, which he always has when he returns from his jobs, but Burt didn't know that. He thought Morgan had escaped from an institution and was there to kill him. Took me a few hours to convince him that Morgan wasn't going to do anything to him."

Robin seemed to relax all the way for the first time since Quinn had dropped the bombshell about knowing he was gay. "So is Morgan gay or straight? Just curious."

"As far as I know, he's straight. He's always had girlfriends and I have to admit he has good taste because most of the women he's dated have been gorgeous and smart. He's gone so much though that none of them have ever managed to stick for longer than a few months. When your boyfriend can disappear without word for months on end, it's hard to keep a relationship going. At some point though, he's going to meet a lady who's going to be strong enough to deal with all the shit his job throws at her. And she'll be the luckiest woman in the world because Morgan's a great guy." Quinn reminded himself to send Morgan a quick email later that night. All the talking about him had Quinn missing his older brother. He stretched and yawned. "I was going to watch a movie. Did you want to join me or are you heading to bed?"

"I'm sort of wound up still. Maybe I'll just sit with you for a while, though I might abandon you if it gets boring." Robin smirked.

"I'm watching *Independence Day*. Will Smith and aliens? How can that get boring?" Quinn wiggled his eyebrows and Robin burst out laughing.

"Okay, you're totally right on that one. Now I have to stay up, at least until the part where Jeff Goldblum walks in slow motion toward the camera. Which is basically at the end anyway."

"Good plan. I'm going to rinse the dishes and put them in the dishwasher. Why don't you go and get the movie set up? I left the DVD on the coffee table." He gathered their plates on his lap then took them over to the sink. He didn't know how Stein or Robin had managed to do it, but they'd found a townhouse to rent for the fortnight that was handicap accessible and the counters in the kitchen were lower, so he could reach them while in his chair.

Robin watched him thoughtfully. "I just noticed how low the counters are. That has to be helpful to you."

"Yeah, it is, especially when I don't feel like wearing my legs." He went about rinsing off the dishes.

After a couple of minutes of quiet, Robin finally retreated to the living room. Quinn finished cleaning up before joining Robin to watch the movie. He confessed to himself he liked the idea of hanging out with Robin as friends and not just as chef and client.

Chapter Twelve

Robin shifted and stifled a sigh just in time. Meditation just wasn't for him. His brain apparently didn't like to turn off, because every time he tried to relax and use the techniques Quinn had taught him, Quinn popped in his head.

What were the chances he'd end up with a gay chef? Robin's eyes popped open. That had just been a rhetorical question but it raised the idea that maybe it hadn't been a coincidence. But if it wasn't, that would mean that either Alfred or Coach...or both...knew about him.

"Robin..." Quinn's eyes were still closed, but somehow he knew that Robin was distracted.

"Sorry." He closed his eyes, did a few cleansing breaths then started his body part by body part relaxation exercise over again. By the time he'd gotten to his shoulders he was back to thinking about Quinn and the image of Danie holding Robin against the wall while Quinn watched. Had it turned him on? The thought of being noticed had freaked him out at first, but in a way it was sort of hot.

Shit, now he was getting turned on. He wriggled a bit to try to adjust his partial erection without being overt about it.

A sigh filtered across the room. When he opened his eyes to peek, Quinn was looking directly at him.

"Sor—"

"Robin, you need to focus."

"I'm trying!" He really was. It wasn't his fault that his mind wanted to go in more pleasurable directions. "Maybe I'll do better when we get home and I can do it in the pool?"

Quinn chuckled. "I swear, you are the antsiest person I've ever met. Okay—we're done for now. How are you feeling about the match today?"

His second round match was this afternoon, and he was feeling pretty good about it. It would be a bigger test of his game since his opponent was seeded and ranked higher than Kroener had been, though. He nodded slowly. "Good. Willer is a solid, methodical player, but I think I can take him."

"You *think* you can take him?"

Robin rolled his eyes but gave a sharp nod. "I *know* I can beat him."

"Much better. I know it might seem silly, but positive thinking can help. Has Ramsey ever done visualization techniques with you?" Quinn stretched in his chair, and a little bit of tan stomach showed below the hem of his T-shirt.

"Um. Probably? I think I remember him using that term before." He tried for cute and innocent but Quinn saw right through him.

"Dude, you know exactly what I'm talking about. You need to visualize winning points on your serves and actually winning games. It'll help. I promise. That's what I did when I wanted to learn to walk again using my prosthetics. I would picture myself wearing them and taking steps with them. It helped me with my confidence and determination." Quinn pointed at him. "Your confidence is one thing that needs help."

All of a sudden an image flashed in Robin's head of Quinn waking up without his legs, trying to walk and falling. He swallowed hard. God, his challenges were nothing compared to this man's. He couldn't believe that Quinn didn't think he was a big joke. He vowed to take everything he was trying to teach him more seriously. "Thank you. You're a big inspiration." And maybe that was exactly why his team had chosen Quinn, not because he was gay. It was harder to discount what someone who'd be through what Quinn had suffered had to say, as opposed to any other mentor.

He got up and walked out of the room before Quinn could respond. It was good to have revelations that might help his mental outlook over the long term, but right before a huge match wasn't exactly ideal. Time for some quiet so he could think about his game and get his head screwed on straight.

* * * *

Robin strode toward the exit, the adrenaline from his win still pumping through his system. He was in Court One again — even though he wasn't seeded in the top four, he was still a media draw, so they always took that into account when scheduling the venues. He passed the door of the room where Danie had gotten him off a couple of days earlier, but of course he wouldn't be there today. He was still finishing his own match, on Centre Court, of course.

Unlike the other day, several people were walking back and forth through the access tunnel. He nodded to people as he passed and clasped hands in a quick greeting with Jerome's former doubles partner, though he didn't stop to chat. Quinn and Ramsey had said they'd be waiting for him...and there they were.

Ramsey pulled him into a back-thumping hug. "Great match, Robin. Way to turn it around."

"Thanks, Coach. It wasn't my best first set ever," he acknowledged.

"Yes, but I could see that your mindset was staying positive even after dropping the first set," Quinn praised him and opened his arms. Robin accepted his hug as well, inhaling his unique scent and enjoying the feel of his firm muscular chest and arms against him.

Quinn shifted from side to side once Robin released him. He was wearing his legs today, and Robin knew they sometimes bothered him, so he started walking toward the car and the other two followed him.

"I think your stamina has improved. You've looked really sluggish from the third set onward in most of your tournaments over the past six months," Ramsey observed. "But I think your new program must be doing you some good."

Robin didn't want to tell his coach that it probably had more to do with the fact that having Quinn stay with him meant that he wasn't drinking. But logically he knew that more focus on his nutrition could do nothing but help.

They reached their car and most of the discussion on the way to the townhouses had to do with Ramsey running down the finer points of his game that he'd observed during the match.

When they pulled up outside their side-by-side townhouses — Ramsey and Jerome were sharing the one next to Robin and Quinn — Robin invited Ramsey in but he declined. "I'm going to do a bit of work and relax for an hour, then I'm heading back. I'd like you to do some stretching as a cool down to stay loose. No workout tonight and don't stay up too late. I'll text you the plan for tomorrow when I confirm our practice court time."

"Okay, Coach."

They said their goodbyes and Quinn and Robin went inside.

"Are you hungry yet?" Quinn asked on his way through the foyer.

"Not even close." He was all hyped up still and whenever he was wound up, he had no appetite. He followed Quinn into the kitchen anyway and grabbed a bottle of water from the fridge.

"Go ahead and hydrate then but you'll need some protein and salt. I'll make a plate of snacks, maybe some cold chicken, almonds and fruit."

"Cheese?" Robin asked hopefully.

"Fine. I'll cube some cheddar as well, but that's not all you're having."

Robin grinned in triumph. As he was leaving the kitchen, his text tone chimed from the foyer. He detoured and pulled it out of the side pocket of his bag. Danie.

Still around?

His match was obviously over. Robin texted back.

No, at the townhouse. You win?

Of course. Guess you're not alone. I won't be seeing you then???

Robin parted his lips. Not only was Quinn keeping him from drinking, he was cock-blocking him. But maybe that wasn't entirely a bad thing. He knew enough to realize that changing a lifestyle didn't just mean one or two parts—everything was usually interrelated. He had a hard time believing that getting together with Danie was a bad thing, but who knew?

No, not alone. Probably not going to happen this tourney.

There was a long enough pause for Robin to walk to his bedroom and sit down on his bed before Danie replied.

No worries. Congrats on your win. Keep it up.

Thanks, you too.

Such a tame conclusion to the exchange considering the unspoken topic, but it gave Robin a lot of food for thought. Once you took sex out of the equation, what did he and Danie really have in common? Tennis...and nothing else. He'd fantasized about being *together* together with Danie for years, but all else being equal, would they work if they had the opportunity to try?

Not wanting to face the finality of the logical answer to that, he quickly changed into lounging clothes—loose sweats and a threadbare T-shirt—which would also work for stretching and meditation later when Quinn thought he was ready for that.

"Movie?" Quinn asked when he got back downstairs. There was a plate of snacks as promised on the coffee table in front of the couch, as well as two glasses of iced tea.

"Sure." He joined Quinn on the couch, noting that Quinn had removed his prosthetic legs and his chair was parked near the other end of the couch. The ends of his legs — Robin hesitated to think of them by the term 'stumps' for some reason — were covered by his sewn-closed sweatpants. He pulled his gaze away. "What are we watching?"

"*The Avengers* all right with you?"

Robin nodded and got up to put in the DVD Quinn handed to him before coming back to sit down. Quinn used the remote to get through the menu and start the movie, and they settled back in a comfortable silence to watch the intro.

No surprisingly, Robin's mind wandered almost immediately. He glanced over at Quinn, watching his profile for a moment. Quinn licked his lips, and it hit Robin suddenly that the attraction he felt toward him might be reciprocated. Quinn was obviously aware of Robin's perusal. He scooted down further on the couch to slouch back and brought his hand to rest on his thigh.

There was no question that Quinn noticed that. Robin could see the sideways flick of his eyes.

Maybe it was a really bad idea to make a move on a man who was, for all intents and purposes, on his staff, but with the victory still pumping him up and the new doubts about where things stood with Danie, he couldn't think of a solid reason not to act on his attraction to Quinn. Of course, Quinn might not welcome it, but he'd never know if he didn't give it a shot.

Gathering all his resolve, he moved quickly to straddle Quinn's lap, twining his fingers with Quinn's as his hands automatically came up to bracket his hips. He gazed into Quinn's eyes, silently pleading with him not to say no.

Chapter Thirteen

Quinn could see the need and want in Robin's eyes, but he couldn't bring himself to kiss him right then. "What about Danie? I thought you guys were together."

As much as it hurt to bring up the other guy's name, Quinn wasn't going to poach his territory just because Robin was horny and happy after winning his second match of the tournament. He tightened his grip on Robin's waist.

"We aren't together. I guess you'd call us fuckbuddies. We hook up at different tournaments. It's not like we go out in public together or anything like that." Robin grimaced. "Not that I want to do that, but it would be nice to have someone acknowledge they want to be with me outside of the bedroom. Danie will never do that."

But that didn't answer whether Robin wanted Danie to. All right. That seemed to be an issue they would have to talk about at some point in the future. Definitely not tonight, though. He let go of Robin to run one of his hands up along Robin's spine to cup the back of his head. "Come here," he whispered then kissed him.

Robin whimpered then rocked his groin into Quinn's and Quinn blocked out where the last time he heard those sounds was. He would deal with the emotions in the morning. They began rubbing against each other while Quinn took the kiss deeper, sliding his tongue along Robin's, tasting the sweetness from the fruit lingering there.

He broke the kiss to take a deep breath before trailing his lips along the line of Robin's neck to the soft skin at the base of his throat. Quinn sucked up a small mark there, suddenly discovering a need to brand Robin as his in some way. Not that anyone but Quinn and Robin would know what the mark was.

"I want you to fuck me," Robin begged with his voice and his body.

Quinn closed his eyes for a second, taking firmer control of his lust. "Christ yes, but we need to go to my room. I'm not quite up to fucking on a couch anymore."

"Why your room?" And before he could explain, Robin rolled his eyes. "Right. Because mine's on the second floor and you'd have to either put your legs back on or scoot up the stairs on your ass."

"And that tends to kill the mood," Quinn confessed, thinking how humiliating it would be to have to do that. Not that Robin would pity him or anything like that, but a man had to have his pride.

"Right."

Robin jumped off his lap then brought Quinn's chair over to where he could get into it easily. When he was settled, he let Robin push him back toward his suite. Any other time he'd tell Robin he could do it himself because being capable was another source of pride for

Quinn, but he was simply interested in getting to his bed as fast as possible.

"Do you have stuff?"

Quinn nodded. "In my kit in the bathroom. Why don't you pull the covers down while I go get it?"

"All right."

Once they were in the bedroom, Robin continued on toward the bed and Quinn took a detour to the bathroom. He dug through his kit until he found the lube and rubbers. He set the items along with a couple of towels in his lap then headed back to Robin.

He stopped next to the mattress where he set the brakes on his chair. He tossed the supplies toward the middle of the bed before swinging himself to join Robin sitting on the edge. Quinn turned to meet Robin's gaze and smiled when Robin leaned in for another kiss. By the time they had to break for air, they were laying side by side facing each other. At some point they'd both lost their T-shirts and sweats.

Quinn hadn't put any underwear on after his shower earlier, so he jerked a little when Robin took a hold of Quinn's cock. There were calluses on Robin's palm and fingers that felt amazing against Quinn's sensitive skin.

"Wow," he murmured, and Robin laughed.

"You think that feels great, just wait." Robin wiggled down to settle between Quinn's thighs.

Bracing himself on his elbows, Quinn looked down to see Robin wink at him before sucking his entire length in. Quinn moaned loudly as the wet heat and suction of Robin's mouth surrounded him. It was better than anything he could've ever imagined. He lost track of time and everything else as Robin worked him with tongue, lips and hands.

As pressure began to build behind his balls, he forced his eyes open and tapped Robin to get his attention. "As much as I love what you're doing, and I really want to come like this some time, if you want me to fuck you, you need to stop."

He could see the struggle in Robin's eyes then he smiled as Robin reluctantly let him slide out of his mouth. Quinn scrambled over the sheets to find the lube. He got the bottle open and some squirted out on his fingers as Robin straddled his hips.

"Is this all right for you?" Robin asked, tracing circles in Quinn's chest hair.

"Yeah. I had some damage to my knees from the same accident that took the lower halves of my legs. Putting any kind of real pressure on them can cause a lot of pain some days." Quinn ran his finger over the wrinkle in Robin's forehead when the man frowned. "Don't worry. If we do it this way, there won't be any pain for either of us and it'll be awesome."

"Fine."

He encouraged Robin to lean forward so he could reach around to finger his hole. Robin inhaled deeply as Quinn pushed one then two fingers in, stretching him. "How's that?" Quinn wasn't interested in causing Robin any pain either. He wanted the entire experience as pleasurable as possible, so Robin would be interested in doing it again.

"I'm good." Robin brushed a kiss over Quinn's lips before pushing back a little, forcing Quinn's fingers in deeper.

He got the clue and began to work Robin's opening, relaxing the ring of muscle to help ease his penetration later. Somehow he managed to hit Robin's gland a few times during the process.

"Quinn...I'm ready," Robin told him.

After removing his fingers and wiping them off on one of the towels, he handed Robin a foil packet. "Put it on me."

Robin shuddered as he tore open the wrapper and Quinn wondered if Robin got off on being ordered around in bed. He certainly didn't like being told what to do in the other aspects of his life. He filed those thoughts away to be examined at another time. He grunted when Robin took his time rolling the latex down over Quinn's length.

"Don't tease, man, or I won't be fucking you," Quinn warned then chuckled at how quickly Robin got the condom settled before coating Quinn's dick with lube.

Quinn placed his hands on Robin's waist to help him balance as he impaled himself on Quinn. They both sighed when Quinn was seated as far in as he could go. Quinn stared up into Robin's brown eyes, seeing how happy the man looked with Quinn's cock in his ass.

"Are you good?"

Robin nodded then rose up, letting Quinn slide from him until just his head was inside before he lowered himself again. The easy rhythm they started with was perfect to learn how well they would move together. As they got more and more in sync, Robin began to move faster until he was almost slamming down onto Quinn.

Grunts and the sound of skin slapping skin filled the air, along with the scent of sweat and lust. The way Robin's ass seemed to be built for Quinn to fill was driving him crazy. He gripped Robin's waist, knowing he was going to leave bruises there, but not caring. The pressure built again and this time he didn't try to stop.

Just as he was about to come, Robin climaxed, spilling cum all over Quinn's abs. The way his inner channel clenched and flexed around Quinn's length drew his own climax from him. He cried out as he flooded the condom.

"Holy shit!"

He rocked his hips the best he could to extend their pleasure as long as possible. It was only when Robin collapsed into his arms that Quinn stilled. He caressed Robin's sweat-drenched hair before placing a kiss on Robin's mouth.

"That was incredible," he praised his lover. "Thank you."

Robin inched away so he could meet Quinn's gaze. "Thank you. I was afraid you'd turn me down."

"Man, I've been jerking off to thoughts of you almost from the moment I met you. There was no way I was going to tell you no when you made the move." He sighed as he felt his softened cock begin to slip out of Robin. "I need to take care of the condom and clean us off."

"Let me. It's easier since I'm on top."

Robin made quick work of the used rubber then wiped them both down with the towels before tossing them as close to the bathroom door as he could get. Quinn held open his arms, offering Robin a place in his embrace. When Robin snuggled close, Quinn smiled. It had been a long time since he'd shared a bed with anyone.

Most of his buddies fucked and ran. It was like they were afraid his amputation was contagious or something. Of course, most of them were still very much into extreme sports and he was a reminder of how things could go to shit in a hurry while rock climbing in a canyon miles away from civilization.

"Why don't we take a nap and when we wake up, I'll make us some dinner while you stretch. That will help not only with the tiredness after the match, but whatever soreness you might have because of the sex." He patted Robin's butt. "We don't want you to regret sleeping with me."

"I don't think I could ever do that," Robin whispered.

That made Quinn feel good on top of the satisfying exhaustion from the sex. He let his eyes drift close while listening to Robin's breathing.

* * * *

"Do I really have to meditate?" Robin pouted when Quinn told him it was time to stretch and meditate after dinner an hour later.

Quinn shook his head. "You know what? Stretch then sit quietly for a while. I don't care if you meditate, just try to not think about too many things at once. This kind of meditation might not be right for you, but I need it."

He settled into his spot in the middle of the living room floor, resting his hands on his thighs. Taking deep breaths, Quinn slowly relaxed each muscle group until all his tension had eased away. Quinn listened to his heart beating and felt the expansion of his chest with each breath in and the collapse with each exhale. It gave him comfort to know all of his body seemed to be working the way it should be. Even the residual aches from the sex made him happy.

Surprisingly Robin managed to stay still for twenty minutes, which was a record for him. When he started twitching, Quinn inhaled and exhaled twice before opening his eyes. He smiled at Robin, who was staring at him like he was memorizing every inch of Quinn's face.

"Are you Greek?"

Blinking at the random question, Quinn thought for a minute. "We must be since our last name is Damaris. I don't know. My parents died when I was two and Morgan was four. He has a few memories of them, but I don't have any. We didn't have any family to take us in, so we stayed in the foster system. When Morgan turned eighteen, he joined the military and left."

"Why did he do that? How could he leave you behind?" Robin looked indignant at what he saw as Quinn's abandonment.

Quinn took Robin's hand in his then tugged the man over to sit at his side. "He left me because right then he had no home for me or any way to support me. I was in a good foster home, so he knew I'd be okay until he could send for me. The day I turned eighteen, he showed up at my doorstep to get me. What I didn't know, and neither did he until he reached twenty, was that our parents had a trust fund for us. We might not remember them but it was obvious they loved us. A lawyer found him and let him know about it. It was enough for us to buy a house in Colorado that I used as my base of operations, though I traveled the world in search of another dangerous sport I could try."

"So you're rich?" Robin teased.

"Not even. I worked a hundred different seasonal jobs wherever I was at the time to get enough money to do whatever it was I wanted to risk my life at." He rubbed his fingers over Robin's knuckles.

Robin took a breath and Quinn knew what was coming. He was surprised that they hadn't talked about it before.

"How did it happen?" Robin barely touched Quinn's stumps as he asked.

Quinn exhaled sharply. "We were young and reckless. Oh, we were careful and experienced enough to do most everything we tried. But we got a little cocky. A group of us were out rock climbing in Arizona." He chuckled at Robin's confused glance. "Yeah. You'd think from the extent of my injuries, we had to be in the outback or something. Nope. Arizona, which is why we got overconfident. It was a place we had climbed in a hundred times."

He thought about that day. After eight years, some of the memories were a little hazy, but he did know what had happened.

"We were about twenty miles out in the desert, having hiked all the way out there with water and ropes. We climbed down into some canyons then one of the belays came loose from where it'd been secured into the rock. I don't know if it was one I set or one that someone else had set. It doesn't matter now. I fell about thirty feet, landing on my feet. Blew out my ankles and broke all the bones in both my lower legs. Compound fractures. Jacked up my knees." He ran his free hand over his thigh. "I was lucky that I didn't break my upper leg bones. I had some broken ribs and a broken right arm."

"Dear God. That's horrible." Robin hugged him close, offering up sympathy. "I'm surprised you survived."

Quinn embraced Robin. "So am I, to be honest. Two of my friends stayed with me while the rest went to get help. It was about three hours before the rescuers and paramedics arrived. I'd been going in and out of consciousness for a while. The pain was incredible. They got me out and to the hospital. The surgeons couldn't do anything to rebuild my ankles and lower legs. There was way too much damage so amputation was their only choice if they wanted me to live."

How much anger had he felt when he'd awoken and realized they had taken his legs? At first it hadn't mattered to him that it had been the only way they could insure he would live. Morgan had done all he could to keep Quinn's morale up.

"I spent a year recovering and when I finally was done with everything, I had two fake legs and a new plan for the rest of my life. Ultimately, the accident put me on a new track that I ended up loving so much better than what I was doing before it." He brushed Robin's hair off his face before kissing him.

There was a hint of saltiness on Robin's lips and Quinn eased back to see Robin was crying. He wiped the tracks from Robin's cheeks.

"Oh don't cry for me. I still get mad from time to time, but I've dealt with the loss. I really am happy with my life right now. Hell, if this hadn't happened to me, I wouldn't be here right now with you." Quinn smiled. "Why don't we share a shower then go to bed and cuddle under the blankets?"

"Sounds good." After standing, Robin brought over his chair for him to climb into.

While Robin headed for the bedroom, Quinn double-checked the locks on the doors before he went to join him. It would be the first time he would spend all night lying in someone's arms and he was looking forward to waking up to see Robin sleeping beside him.

Chapter Fourteen

"Robbie, you've got to stop being so hard on yourself. So you lost in the third round. That's a damn good showing, actually, considering how your year had been going to crap."

"Not helping," Robin growled into the phone at Danie. He shot a glance sideways at Quinn, sitting quietly next to him in the back of the car on their way to Heathrow. Ramsey was staying behind to coach Jerome, so it would just be the two of them for at least the next week.

"Grass is not your best surface and you withdrew from all of the grass court run-up tourneys this month—which I totally understand," Danie continued, undeterred. "But you came in to Wimbledon cold and on a losing streak and *still* won your first two handily. You've had fantastic years where you got beat in the same damn round at Wimbledon, so don't act like this is a huge set back."

"Don't you have your own damn match to think about?" He knew he shouldn't have answered the phone. Bad habit he needed to break.

"Look, *brah*," Danie soothed, "I just wanted to make sure you're in a decent headspace since you're going home alone."

"I'm not alone—I have Quinn with me," he returned automatically. Quinn turned to face him but didn't say anything.

"Oh." There was a long pause. "That's good then. I suppose I was worried for nothing."

Robin sighed. "I appreciate it, but I'm just... Don't I have the right to be disappointed? Who the fuck *likes* to lose? It's a bit much to expect for me to be all Zen and philosophical about it. God knows you'd be pissed off if you lost to Grigor Dimitrov after beating him two times out of three."

"More like every time," Danie corrected.

"Bite me."

"You wish." Danie growled in frustration. "God, listen to me. I'm starting to sound like you."

The disgust in Danie's tone made him laugh when he wouldn't have thought it was possible. "You're finally loosening up," he teased, then shot a glance at Quinn when he shifted in his seat. The tense set to his jaw clued him in that he was being rude and should wrap up the conversation. "Hey, I appreciate the pep talk but I really have to go. Good luck with the rest of your matches."

"Thanks, Robbie. Work hard and be good...and by that I mean, lay off the sauce." Danie's voice had dropped to a whisper for the last part. "I'll see you back on the tour, yeah?"

"Yeah. I'm not sure where I'm jumping back in"— and Coach and Alfred hadn't sat down with him and gone over the July schedule yet—"but I definitely don't want to go into the US Open as cold as this one."

"That I agree with. Probably good you took this break, but unless you screw up your knee again, you need to be playing. There'll be enough times you have to sit out for injuries."

Wasn't that the truth? Robin made a vow to call Coach as soon as he got home to lobby for going back to his full-time schedule.

"Anyway, I'm off then. Take care, Robbie."

"You too. Bye."

"Goodbye." Danie disconnected.

Robin replaced his phone into his pocket as casually as he could, very aware that Quinn had overheard every bit of his conversation, with the possible exception of the whispered admonishment about his drinking. It was a pretty awkward situation—having slept with Quinn, who knew about him and Danie, then taking a call from the 'other man' in front of him.

Well, it wasn't like they were dating or anything. He wasn't really answerable to Quinn, or Danie, for that matter.

"Sorry about that. He doesn't call all that often, so I figured I should see what was up."

Quinn's eyebrows drew inward then he relaxed. "You can talk to anyone you like, Robin. It sounded like it was a good call, that he cared how you were doing and wanted to give you a boost."

"Yeah, pretty much. I mean, there's no one who knows what it's like on tour and in tournaments like someone in the same situation."

"I understand." There was a flat tone to Quinn's voice that had Robin jerking his head to the side to look at him. His jaw flexed.

Robin mentally ran through what he'd just said. *Fuck.* "Hey—I really appreciate *your* support as well. I didn't mean anything more than... Danie just knows what it's like to play the same guys, be under the same intense scrutiny. We share a lot of experiences in common. But I'm glad you're here." He chanced a light touch to Quinn's thigh. "You've helped me a lot."

"That's my job."

That short answer landed like an unexpected punch and Robin yanked his hand away as hurt flooded his chest, making it hard to breathe.

"Damn it." Quinn sighed heavily. "I didn't mean it that way. Robin?"

"Wha—" He cleared his throat and tried again. "What?"

"This is complicated, because we have more between us now. But you know that helping you return to your best competitive level *is* my job. It's what I'm trained for and what I'm good at. That's all I meant."

They'd both been facing forward during the majority of the conversation. Robin angled himself in his seat so he could look directly at Quinn, who gazed back at him searchingly.

"I guess neither one of us is doing a good job at communicating right now. How about we table any talk about Danie, your job or tennis until we're home and rested?"

"I second the motion. So, you think we'll find other topics of conversation?" Quinn's voice was back to normal and it did wonders to help calm Robin down as well.

"I don't think that's ever been a problem," he answered truthfully. Whereas his dealings with Danie were still strictly sex or tennis even after years of knowing one another, in just a month, Robin had reached a level of comfort with Quinn that he couldn't ever remembering sharing with another guy.

And *that* was definitely something to think about on the flight home...if he and Quinn ever ran out of things to talk about.

Somehow he doubted there would be time to ponder it today.

* * * *

Their trip home had been mostly uneventful. To his embarrassment, Robin had fallen asleep on the flight, but Quinn had reassured him that he hadn't snored or otherwise made a fool of himself. It had felt great to walk into his house, more so than it usually did after leaving a tournament early.

They'd headed immediately into the kitchen — Quinn's domain — where Margerite had greeted them with a light snack and shown Quinn that she'd stocked the fridge and pantry for him.

"Margerite, you're the best."

Robin grinned at the pleased flush his housekeeper wore at Quinn's compliment. He'd noticed that they had formed a mutual admiration society, which was fine with him. His smile dropped a bit as it occurred to him for the first time that Quinn wasn't here permanently — had only agreed to an initial three months, one of which was gone already. It was sort of sad how quickly Robin had gone from resenting his presence to craving it.

He snorted. He supposed having had amazing sex with the man didn't hurt.

It's not just his presence you crave...

"Don't be cheeky. I just followed the shopping list you prepared. Anyone could do that." She flapped a hand in his direction.

Quinn immediately glanced at him in inquiry, and after a moment, Robin clued in and gave Quinn a quick translation. Margerite spoke French and German almost exclusively, and though she did know some English, she understood it much better than she spoke it. Since Quinn had the same sort of limited facility with French, it made their conversations somewhat basic and occasionally amusing, but they made it work. Usually.

Margerite turned to Robin. "Anke and I, we have little to do today since you've been gone, so…"

"Go ahead. We can fend for ourselves."

"Yes, well, I believe that's true with Quinn here." She switched from French to German to whisper, "The household is much better with him here. I hope he stays here for a long time."

Since that sentiment echoed his thoughts, he wasn't ashamed to agree wholeheartedly, "*Ich auch.*"

After Margerite and Anke had left for the day, Quinn went into his bedroom to shower and change out of his prosthetics. So Robin wandered upstairs with some vague idea about cleaning up.

The idea formed that at this moment, they had the house truly to themselves. The women wouldn't be back until tomorrow, Alfred was at home in the States and Jerome and Coach were still in England. Now that he and Quinn had figured out their mutual attraction, the absolute privacy took on a more intimate slant.

Make-out sessions on the couch. Blow jobs in the kitchen. Swimming with Quinn in the nude.

As the possibilities rapidly flipped through his mind, his cock began to respond, especially when he thought about Quinn, naked and wet in the shower downstairs.

What the hell was he waiting for?

Robin stripped off all of his clothes, scattering them across his room as he headed toward the hallway then pounded down the stairs. It was an odd feeling walking through the house without any clothes on, but it heightened his arousal to feel the cool air on his heated flesh.

At Quinn's bedroom door, which was mostly shut, he paused and a bit of the wind left his sails. Did he dare invade Quinn's privacy on the basis of one sexual encounter? That was really crossing all sorts of lines...

"Looking for me?"

Robin yelled and spun around to see Quinn in his chair behind him. "Dammit! Oh God, you almost gave me a heart attack." He remembered he was nude and dropped his hands automatically to cover his groin. Well, mostly anyway. His cock was a bit hard to hide at the moment.

"Sorry." Quinn didn't look it. He ran his gaze slowly over Robin's body, and Robin relaxed, letting his arms fall back to his sides, giving Quinn the full show.

"You can come to my door anytime if you keep bringing me presents like that."

A smile spread Robin's mouth then he started laughing. "I thought you might like it."

Quinn moved closer. There was something rather erotic about being naked while Quinn was fully clothed.

"Did you take a shower?" Robin asked then his breath caught as Quinn reached out and took his cock in hand.

"Not yet. Thought we might take a swim...after."

"A-after what?" The firm grip and sure strokes were making Robin's brain turn to mush and his knees weak.

"After we christen the kitchen." Quinn let go of Robin's shaft and he groaned in frustration. Taking himself in hand, he pumped lightly as he watched Quinn unzip a toiletries bag he'd just noticed was on Quinn's lap. He must have gone to retrieve it from his suitcase in the foyer.

"I like how you think," Robin managed as Quinn pulled out lube and a condom.

"I thought you might. Looks like you might have had the same idea." Quinn didn't wait for confirmation. He patted Robin's flank. "Go to the table."

Robin hurried to comply. He raised an eyebrow at Quinn.

"Turn around and bend over. Make yourself comfortable."

"Oh God." Robin moved into position, resting his head on his forearms, hyperaware of Quinn coming up behind him while everything was exposed to his gaze. Instead of embarrassment, he was flushed with arousal.

The first slick, glancing touch to his hole made him moan, the sound loud in the quiet house.

"Yeah. I like to hear you. Don't stifle it." Quinn stroked him until he was arching back then finally rewarded him with a couple of fingers, dipping shallow at first then deeper. With how turned on Robin had been since before he came downstairs, it didn't take long for Quinn to bring him teetering close to the edge, especially after he starting paying particular attention to his prostate. It wasn't a hard massage, but glancing nudges that made him rock back for more.

"Quinn...God...please touch me."

"My pleasure." He reached under Robin and gave him the much needed contact he'd been craving. Instead of grasping his cock, though, he used the palm of his hand to give Robin a slick surface to thrust against. The teasing touch mirrored his light movements inside, and Robin was panting and moaning like crazy now, chasing more, needing more.

"Oh no." Robin gasped when Quinn removed his fingers, then thankfully he was penetrated again, this time accompanied by fingers cupping his sac. His balls tightened at the touch. *He has his thumb in me.* For some reason, that was totally hot and he spread his stance restlessly. The move must have sent a message to Quinn, because he finally gripped Robin's aching cock and jacked it hard.

Robin came with a throaty yell. Quinn petted him through his climax and aftershocks, not removing his touch, just lightening the pressure until he was sagging with repletion.

The sound of the condom wrapper penetrated his satiated fog. He made an inquiring noise in his throat and straightened up.

"I want you to sit on my cock. So stay facing that direction and put your hands here." Quinn patted the arms of his chair.

Once he had lightly gripped the arms where Quinn had indicated, he looked over his shoulder. Quinn was adding lube to his sheathed erection then held the base with one hand and stroked Robin's lower back and ass with the other.

"Ready?"

"Oh yeah." Robin braced himself and, as Quinn guided his movements, lowered himself until the head of Quinn's cock was notched against his entrance. He pushed out as he let gravity work and Quinn popped inside.

"Hold on." His back was stroked soothingly. "Take it slow."

"Screw that." He let himself sink back and took Quinn inside in one smooth motion until he was sitting on his lap.

"Fuck. Don't hurt yourself," Quinn gritted out.

"Mmm. Doesn't hurt. Well, not in the bad way." He rocked his pelvis, still using his hands to control the amount of weight he had on Quinn, who took his hips in his large hands.

It took a bit of trial and error at first to settle into a rhythm, since the chair was a bit confining, but Robin took his time and tried to make it as pleasurable as possible for Quinn. He was soon rewarded with a harsh groan.

"God! So hot." Quinn dug his fingers into Robin's hips and held him still as he pulsated inside Robin.

Robin opened eyes he hadn't realized he'd closed and found he could see the two of them in the reflection of the window. *Wow.* "So hot is right."

And the week was just beginning. Usually he had a hard time settling in after getting home from a trip, but Robin knew he'd sleep well that night. Especially if Quinn didn't mind Robin joining him in his bed.

Chapter Fifteen

"Hey, Ace."

Quinn turned carefully when he heard Morgan call out to him. Grinning, he watched his brother wind his way through the crowd at the National Tennis Center right outside Arthur Ashe stadium. God, he had missed his brother. They had talked every week while Quinn had been out of the country, but it wasn't the same as seeing Morgan face-to-face.

Morgan caught him in a tight hug, squeezing all the air out of his lungs before letting him go. Quinn smiled up at his big brother.

"You're looking good. Hanging out at my place seems to agree with you," he said as he motioned for Morgan to follow him. "I thought we could grab a cab and go into the city to get something to eat."

"Don't you need to stick around with Keller?" Morgan fell in stride with him easily.

Quinn lifted one shoulder in a halfhearted shrug. "He's doing some hitting with Jerome, then working out with his coach. After that he has some media thing. He said he'd text me when he was done and we'd catch up. Did you want to meet him?"

Morgan snorted. "Is that a trick question? Hell yes, I want to meet the guy my brother's sleeping with."

Morgan's statement caused Quinn to freeze then glare at him. "What the fuck, Morgan? Can we not talk about it here?" He waved his hands wildly as he tried to encompass the entire complex. "You don't know who might be listening."

"So you're not denying it?" Morgan nudged Quinn to get him moving again.

"No, I won't lie to you. Plus, hell, as spooky as you are, you probably knew the moment we hit the bed together," he joked, though he wasn't happy about Morgan bringing it up in public like that. No matter how he felt about the whole situation, he wasn't interested in taking the chance of ruining Robin's career by outing him.

"Ew! Can we not actually talk about your sex life? I don't want to think about my baby brother having sex with anyone. It's just too squicky for me." Morgan shuddered as he flagged down a cab. "I know a great steak place near here. I'll pay and you can tell me what has you concerned about this relationship or whatever it is you've got going."

Quinn wasn't about to say no to a free steak, and knowing Morgan like he did, the restaurant would be classy and expensive, but not too highbrow. Morgan's job sent him all over the world and gave him a chance to go places that two orphans from Colorado rarely would've seen on their own. That was one of the reasons why Quinn chose to do what he did—aside from being good at it—being a live-in chef gave him opportunities to travel and visit countries he might not have been able to visit before.

"Sounds good to me."

Twenty minutes later, they were pulling up in front of a nondescript building and getting out. He allowed Morgan to take the lead and before he knew it, they were seated at a private table in the corner of the restaurant. Morgan ordered for them, and Quinn didn't see the point in arguing. His brother had a tendency to take over sometimes, which often irritated him no end, but he wasn't concerned about asserting his independence at the moment.

After their drinks had been delivered, Morgan leaned back in his chair, crossed his legs and studied Quinn. "What's got you worried about this relationship?"

"The fact that I think he's been having some kind of weird relationship with this other tennis player."

"You mean he's cheating on you already?" Morgan had stiffened, almost as though he were ready to leap to his feet and defend Quinn's honor.

"No," Quinn said then paused for a second. When he spoke again, even he could hear the hesitation in his voice. "I think they might have done something at Wimbledon while we were there, but I don't think he's actually slept with Danie since the French. We didn't get together until a couple of days before we left England."

"You don't *think*?" Morgan shook his head. "Tell me what the hell is going on, Quinn. You've never been the guy to settle for being second fiddle to anyone."

Quinn stared at the water in his glass while he tried to organize the thoughts meandering in his head. "I caught Robin and Danie together at Wimbledon."

Morgan took a swig of his beer before saying, "*Together* together?"

"No. Just a kiss, but it was obvious that they were more than just good friends. I mean after the kiss, they disappeared together. I didn't follow to find out where they went." Quinn laughed. "It's silly really because I wasn't even the one to make the first move. Robin did, and I know him well enough that if he were in a serious relationship with Danie, he wouldn't have even thought about doing anything with me."

"Yet you can't get that kiss out of your mind," Morgan commented.

Nodding, Quinn sighed. "I know it's stupid, Morgan, but I can't help thinking that I'm just a guy he's using to scratch an itch. That Danie is the one he really wants, but can't have for some reason."

Morgan reached over to flick Quinn on the forehead.

"Ow! What was that for?" He rubbed the injured spot as he growled at Morgan.

"Your problem is that you think Robin deserves Danie because he deserves a whole man. Not one who doesn't have his legs anymore. This has nothing to do with what Robin wants or doesn't want. And everything to do with your insecurities." Morgan grimaced. "I thought we'd talked about this before. You're still the amazing guy you were before the accident. Actually, you're even more awesome because of what you've had to overcome."

Quinn couldn't help but smile. Morgan had been his biggest cheerleader from the instant he'd woken up in the hospital after the amputations. He'd been there pushing and helping Quinn through his long rehab then encouraging him when he chose to go to culinary school. As far as Morgan was concerned, Quinn was a superhero, as he'd told him several times over the years.

"I know all that and it's not like I haven't dated guys since my injuries. This doesn't have anything to do with me being an amputee. I really do believe that once Robin gets back on the tour regularly and starts winning again—and I'm not needed anymore—he'll dump me for Danie." Quinn stopped talking as the waiter approached to deliver their dinners.

Morgan also waited until after the man left before he asked, "If you believe that, then why even sleep with him? You can get your rocks off with some other guy, I'm sure."

Rolling his eyes, Quinn grunted. "Seriously? Get my rocks off?"

Shrugging, Morgan didn't say anything, motioning for Quinn to continue.

"Fine. I sleep with him because I really like him. He's funny and nice. And let's not forget how fucking hot he is." Quinn shifted in his seat as his cock began to fill at the memory of what they'd done in their suite the night before. They'd been going hot and heavy ever since they'd broken the ice between them after Wimbledon. "He's not perfect by any means, and we're working on some of his deeper issues, but I like spending time with him, not just in bed. I like to think we're not just lovers, we're friends and that's important to me. He isn't a job to me anymore. I want him to succeed because I care about him, not how it will look on my resume."

He watched Morgan take a couple of bites of his steak and chew before responding to him.

"I guess if you're willing to sleep with him, even though you think he's going to dump you in the end, then you're a braver man than me, Ace. I wouldn't risk the heartache." Morgan tapped Quinn's hand with his finger. "I'll be there to pick up the pieces if it comes to that, but why not have some hope? Maybe it won't turn out that way and he'll choose you over that other guy."

Quinn didn't think that would happen, but he'd already told himself he would ride the Robin rollercoaster for as long as it lasted. He was going to get Robin back into top condition and winning Grand Slams before he left, then he'd let him go, if that was what Robin wanted. *Such a good little martyr.*

"Enough about my love life. I want to know what happened during your last mission and why you've been so fucked up about it."

Morgan chuckled. "You need to pick a different subject if you're trying to change the one we're on. You know I can't talk about my job."

"All right. What have you been doing since I left?"

Quinn settled in to listen to the list of improvements Morgan had made to Quinn's house in his absence. As nervous as he was about Morgan meeting Robin, he did want the two men he cared most about in the world to get to know each other. Hopefully Morgan would give Robin the benefit of the doubt.

* * * *

It was the first sit-down interview Alfred had approved for Robin since everything had started going south last year. Sure, he'd had the usual post-match press conferences, but nothing where he'd be on display from a studio in street clothes while having a list of questions ahead of time to prepare for. They all could only hope the interviewer stuck to the script.

Coach hadn't been completely certain that this was the way to go, but Alfred had been adamant that Robin take the opportunity to refocus some of the negative press he'd gotten over the past year. The last thing he wanted, he'd said, was for them to look like they were avoiding putting Robin in front of the camera.

The makeup artist gave him one last dusting of powder then removed the cape. "Ready for mic," she told the technician impatiently hovering to one side.

"Finally," he muttered and urged Robin to stand while he got the wiring situated to his satisfaction. He led Robin like a dog on a leash over to the set, where two cozy chairs were set at an angle, with a table between and a fireplace in the background.

After he was seated and more fiddling with the mic, they asked him to say something for a sound check.

Great. "What should I say?"

Another guy rolled his eyes. "That's fine. That's basically what everyone says. Are we good?" he called over to someone out of view behind Robin then gave a thumbs-up. "Okay. Sit tight. You need some water?"

"Please."

"Water!" he yelled and soon a very young-looking woman hurried over with two bottles of water, handed Robin one and left the other one on the table, presumably for his interviewer. He didn't have one of the big names in tennis coverage doing the interview, which was fine with him—they were always a bit intimidating. This was evidently going to be a 'We caught up with Robin earlier and here's what he had to say' type of thing to show probably during the warm-ups for his first match.

He tried not to fidget then took a long drink of water, barely keeping from dripping it onto his polo shirt. Setting the bottle down before he could mess anything up, he went back to mentally reviewing the questions and answers.

"Hello, Robin. Good to meet you." Jacob Hunter shook with him then settled into his own chair, ignoring the technicians buzzing around him with the air of long practice.

"You too." Robin closed his eyes to think. They'd told him not to over-prepare so it didn't sound rehearsed, but some of the topics were tough, so he'd had multiple text exchanges with Alfred clarifying the best things to say. Now he just had to remember them when the time came.

"A little bit of extra celebrating last night, huh?"

Robin's eyes flew open. "Excuse me?" What popped into his head was the way Quinn and he had spent their evening, rubbing off together on the couch.

"Drinking? Might want to rein that in during the Open."

The knowing look in Hunter's eyes began to unravel Robin's confidence, but it also pissed him off. He hadn't had a drink since he'd gotten to the States for the tournament before this one, and even at home he was sober. He'd effectively gone cold turkey since his habitual time of day to enjoy a few vodka rocks was right before bed, and now he had company during that time. Surprisingly, especially considering his family history with his birth mother's alcoholism, he didn't really miss it. He still took the Soma to help unwind or if his body ached, but the drinking had all but stopped.

He knew he was probably damned if he did and damned if he didn't, but he found himself refuting the implication. "No, nothing like that. I was just thinking about the list of questions that you cleared with Alfred."

The not-so-subtle reminder for Jacob to stick to the script didn't produce any reaction other than a smirk. "Ready to get started then?"

"I think so." He ran his palms restlessly along his thighs.

Jacob gave him a reassuring smile that somehow managed to look friendly and fake at the same time. "I won't say don't be nervous, because a little bit of nerves translates well on camera. Just speak clearly, and remember—we're not live, so we can edit if we need to."

That reminder helped to settle Robin's nerves quite a bit, actually, so he took a few deep breaths while they finished getting Jacob ready then made one more pass at him. Lights came up and the temperature rose almost immediately. Hopefully they could wrap this up before he started visibly sweating. Problem was, after this he might be meeting Quinn's brother for the first time. Talk about nerve-racking. They barely knew what they had going between them, and now he had to meet the family?

Guiltily, he thought about his parents. He'd been so involved with Quinn during his at-home time bracketing the couple of ATP tournaments he'd played in between Wimbledon and now that he'd only gotten over to see them once. Not good. He made a mental note to call them his next free morning.

A burst of activity brought his focus back and the director counted them down.

"I'm here with tenth seeded Robin Keller. Robin, thanks for joining me today."

"Thank you for having me," he responded, thankful that his voice seemed clear.

"Robin is one of a group of young, up-and-coming men, including Novak Djokovic, Danie Coetzee and

Grigor Dimitrov, looking to dethrone the long-reigning kings of the sport, Rafael Nadal and Robin's fellow countryman, Roger Federer. You've been likened more to Nadal than Federer, however. What do think about that comparison?"

"Well, it's an honor, of course. Nadal is an incredible player and competitor." He left his modest reply at that. Robin had to work to keep his expression neutral since every single time he played, the announcers brought up the Nadal angle.

Jacob got an almost theatrically serious look on his face that told Robin the tougher part of the conversation was about to hit. After his snarky jab about drinking before they'd started, Robin tensed, bracing for the worst.

Leaning forward and clasping his hands together, Jacob changed gears. "This has been a tough year for you. After what had to be a disappointing second round defeat in the Australian, you had spotty showings in various tournaments."

He paused and Robin didn't know if he was supposed to say something or what, since he'd hadn't actually asked a question.

Thankfully after a moment he moved on. "Then came your shocking first round loss at *your* venue, Roland Garros, on your best surface. Stojanović admittedly played a good tournament at the French, but you must have expecting a win going into that match."

"Yeah. I got off to a bad start, and Stojanović didn't make any errors for me to capitalize on to turn it around." Robin didn't have to fake his discomfort and disappointment at hearing his failure summed up. He launched into his prepared redirection. "It was definitely a turning point in my season."

"Yes, a lot changed for you after that. I understand that your team brought in noted personal chef, Quinn Damaris. So they felt that your diet or health was partially at fault for your struggles?"

"Partially," he allowed. "I think there comes a time when you've been traveling and playing so much, and you concentrate on the same training and workouts. Sometime you need to change things up in areas that you might not have thought about before."

Justin beamed at him, leaning back. "Well, it's hard to argue with the results so far. You had a much better showing at Wimbledon, and then quarter-final and semi-final appearances at the other tournaments you've played this summer. How are you feeling going into the Open tomorrow?"

"Really good." He tried to project confidence. "I'm feeling strong and rested and ready to play." *And I haven't been drinking, asshole.*

"Well, we're all looking forward to seeing what you can do. Thank you for joining us, Robin, and good luck."

"Thank you, Jacob."

He waited while Jacob then recorded a couple of different endings, presumably to play at different times or maybe they hadn't decided when to use it—one where he said viewers could see Robin in action tomorrow, and another where he sent it back to the commentator courtside at Robin's first round match.

Robin sat tight until it was all done then let the technicians untangle him before he once again shook with Jacob. "Thanks again. I appreciate it."

"You did great. I look forward to our follow-up after your tournament has run its course, whenever that might be."

"Follow-up?" Robin repeated, not getting what he meant.

Jacob gave him a sly smile. "Yes, the second interview your team promised me in return for not going off-script during this one."

Oh great. "I see." He supposed he should be grateful to Alfred for making sure he didn't get bashed before the Open, but he really wasn't looking forward to having to do this again after he either lost or won the whole thing. Just gave him more incentive to play his ass off. "Well, I'll be talking to you again next week or the week after, then." He hoped.

"Confidence. I like that. Hope your play backs it up. Maybe next time we can talk about just what you've been doing to manage the residual pain from your knee injury. I'm sure the world would be interested to hear about that." Jacob smirked after dropping that bombshell, his implication clear.

Fuck.

"Good luck tomorrow, Robin." He turned and strode off-set, leaving Robin standing staring after him.

Somehow he knew about what Robin had been doing—the drinking and, it seemed, the Soma use. Not that he'd been doing much of it lately. Between traveling and spending so much time in tight proximity with Quinn, he hadn't been able to…

Robin froze. No. That was the wrong way to put it. He hadn't *needed* to drink or rely on the painkillers. He still had part of the bottle that Jerome had given him before Wimbledon. And he rarely drank anymore, certainly not daily like he had been when his career had been circling the drain.

But the fact that he wasn't currently doing anything counter to his training didn't mean that it wouldn't cause a media nightmare if it came out—especially about the Soma and how he kept getting hold of it. It wasn't like he was using a performance enhancer like steroids or anything, but even the hint of an addiction or wrongdoing would put him under a great deal of scrutiny and further undermine his reputation.

Danie only knew about the drinking, not the pills, and vice versa with Jerome. No one knew the whole scope of the real reason he'd hit such a losing streak. The fact that he was better now wouldn't matter. He'd really thought that his way of dealing with the stress was his business alone, especially once he'd sort of weaned himself off them both.

Now it was coming back to bite him, and he had to figure out how to head this guy off—either that or man up and tell Coach and Alfred the truth and hope they could help him come up with a plan.

Thinking about the looks on their faces made Robin feel a little ill. His parents, too. They would be so upset. After losing Robin's mother to alcohol poisoning, they were adamant teetotalers.

And Quinn? Robin couldn't begin to imagine his disappointment in him.

The thing was, who in Robin's inner circle had leaked the info? He wasn't a party animal. He did his drinking alone at home almost exclusively, that or in hotel rooms on his own. And Jerome was the only one who knew about the pills. Well, Jerome and his source, but Robin was pretty sure they wouldn't have said anything since they were involved. Or would they have? Who else was there and why would they do such a thing?

He blew out a breath then pulled out his phone to text Quinn as he left the studio.

Done. Where should I meet you and Morgan?

Time to put this aside if he could and face his second — and in some ways tougher — interview of the evening.

Chapter Sixteen

Done. Where should I meet you and Morgan?

Quinn glanced over at Morgan after reading the text. "Robin's done. You still want to meet him?"

Morgan shot him a *'duh'* look. "Yes, Quinn. I still want to meet your boyfriend."

Rolling his eyes, Quinn typed in a reply.

We're done as well. Meet you at the suite in twenty?

"We'll meet back at the hotel. I think this meeting should be private in case you piss Robin off." He flagged down a cab. "Plus I want to get my prosthetics off."

They climbed into the back of the cab and he gave the driver the name of their hotel. Once they were settled, Morgan huffed.

"What makes you think I'll upset Robin? I'm a nice guy."

"If I believed that, you'd be able to convince me that the moon is made of cheese. You are obnoxious and arrogant, Morgan. If you think Robin isn't right for me, you'll do all you can to get him to break up with me."

"Break up with you? Are you in high school now? Did you give him your class ring?" Morgan snickered.

Quinn punched him in the arm. "Shut the fuck up. You know what you're like and not everyone is willing to put up with your bullshit."

His phone vibrated and he checked the text.

Cool. Meet you there.

After stuffing his phone in his pocket, he wiped his suddenly damp palms on his thighs. He cleared his throat to get Morgan's complete attention.

"What's wrong, Ace? You have to know I won't mess with him. I get that you really like him. I just want to make sure he's good enough for you."

"Good enough? He's one of the top tennis players in the world and probably the hottest man out there. How could he not be good enough for me?" Quinn shook his head.

Morgan blinked. "Since when are you so shallow that looks and money are the only thing you care about?"

"Fuck. I don't care about them. I was just saying."

"Little brother, while I agree with your assessment of Robin's ability and looks, I'm more interested in his intelligence and personality. Also, how he treats you is more important than his bank balance." Morgan smirked. "Besides, I already know his past history."

Quinn glared at his brother. "You did a background check on him?"

Morgan shrugged. "Sure I did. I do that every time you get a new client. I like knowing who my little brother is working for."

"You just don't want me to end up working for some drug cartel or mob boss," Quinn replied.

"What kind of big brother would I be if I let you get involved in shit like that?"

"True." He looked out of the window as they pulled up in front of the hotel. "Here we go."

He waited on the sidewalk while Morgan paid the cabbie. Once that was done, he led the way into the lobby over to the elevators. Robin had gotten them a two-bedroom suite, even though they only used one.

They got in the elevator and Quinn pushed the fourteenth floor button. "Do you have a place to stay in the city or did you want to crash with us?"

"I got a room closer to the airport. I don't want to cramp your style." Morgan wiggled his eyebrows suggestively.

His cheeks heated and Quinn couldn't believe he was blushing. It had been years since Morgan had teased him enough to embarrass him. "Okay. I just wanted to make sure. We do have an extra room if you wanted to stay here."

Morgan clapped him on the shoulder. "No problem, Quinn. I actually have some business to take care of near my hotel, so staying where I am is fine."

When they got off on Quinn's floor, he headed to his room. He unlocked the door then opened it. Morgan slipped past him to check the suite, and Quinn let him, used to the way his brother always cleared every room before he allowed Quinn inside.

"Come on in," Morgan called.

He walked in to find his brother standing by the window. "I'm taking these off. I'll be back in a few.

You can get a drink or something." He motioned toward the mini bar before he went into the master bedroom.

Quinn grabbed some sweats out of the dresser along with a long-sleeved T-shirt. After arranging his chair next to the bed, he stripped off his jeans then removed his prosthetics. He placed them to the side, wanting them close in case they decided to go out later on. It took a little while to change his clothes before going back out to the living room again.

Morgan was sprawled on the couch, a glass of whiskey in his hand. He smiled at Quinn, and for the first time, Quinn focused on his brother.

"You're not sleeping again," he remarked.

"It'll happen when it happens. I've learned not to force it." Morgan seemed casual about his insomnia. "It's one of the drawbacks of my job."

And they didn't discuss Morgan's job ever, so Quinn decided to not to talk at all. It was nice to be with someone who'd known him all his life. Morgan understood the silence between them and didn't feel the need to fill it.

They both looked up when the door opened and Quinn didn't comment on the fact that Morgan had slid his hand toward his back. His brother always had a weapon on him, so it didn't surprise him. He smiled as Robin entered the suite.

"Hey there," Quinn said as he went to meet Robin.

He saw Robin shoot Morgan a nervous glance, but when Quinn took his hand to tug him down, he relaxed a bit and smiled. He brushed a kiss over Quinn's mouth before straightening.

"It's nice to meet you, Morgan." He offered his hand to Morgan, who rose before accepting it to shake.

Quinn rolled his eyes at Morgan's obvious power play, not wanting to remain seated while Robin stood over him.

"I've heard a lot about you." The slight stress on *lot* wasn't overt but it was there.

When Robin narrowed his eyes a touch, Quinn quickly intervened. "How was your interview?"

Diverted, Robin made a sour face then sighed heavily as he dropped onto the couch. "It went okay, but I'm going to pay for that."

Quinn couldn't quite figure that one out. Morgan also wore a puzzled look.

"Alfred...my manager," he clarified in an aside to Morgan, "made a deal with the interviewer. In return for not throwing me any curveballs, he gets another crack at me after I'm done with the Open, whether it's tomorrow or after the final." He looked almost ill at the thought.

Quinn leaned over to take his hand. "Are you worried about this guy? I'm not sure what he could ask you that would freak you out."

Robin bit his bottom lip as he stared at Quinn and he got the feeling there was definitely something Robin wanted to tell him. Morgan grunted, drawing both of their gazes, and knowing his brother so well, Quinn got it that Morgan knew what questions the interviewer could ask him.

"Are you going to tell me what's got you freaked out or do I have to ask my brother?"

"What?" Robin shot a wild-eyed glance between him and Morgan. "How would he know anything?"

"I have access to better equipment to do background checks," Morgan bragged, though he didn't look particularly happy about it.

"What is it?"

Robin shook his head. "I need to talk to Alfred, Coach, and you at the same time. I don't want to go over this more than once."

"You're going to tell?" Morgan sounded impressed. "Good for you."

Quinn hated not knowing what was going on, but he understood about Robin not wanting to repeat it. He shouldn't have been surprised that Morgan knew all of Robin's secrets. Hell, he'd probably known Robin was gay before Quinn did.

"Oh, I'm so glad you're proud of me." Robin's tone was snarky. "I'm not sure what I would do without your approval."

Morgan opened his mouth and Quinn didn't want the two men he cared most about getting into a shouting match. He touched Robin's hand again. "Are you hungry? We can get something from room service."

"Really? Didn't you tell me that room service wasn't ever on my diet again?" Robin clung to Quinn's hand as though he needed to be anchored somehow.

"You can order healthy food from there, just need to ask for it." Quinn motioned to Morgan. "The menu is on the end table next to you."

Morgan snatched it up then tossed it over at Quinn who caught it. Quinn pointed to the couch. "Why don't you sit and chat with Morgan while I order you something? Be nice to each other."

He went to the desk to dial room service and while he waited for them to answer, he watched Robin and Morgan. Quinn wondered what they were talking about as Morgan leaned closer to Robin. Once he'd ordered, he rolled his chair back over to them.

"What's it like standing at Centre Court and talking to the Duke of Kent while holding that trophy for the first time?" Morgan asked and Quinn had a feeling that he was changing the subject.

"It's amazing. One of those moments I dreamed about when I was young. It was one of the reasons why I left my family and moved to Florida to train with my coach." Robin smiled. "I was so excited but also nervous about meeting the duke."

"Does it get old after you've won a couple majors? Turn into just another win?" Morgan took a sip of his drink.

"Not the Grand Slam tournaments. Those never get boring. That's why this losing streak I've been on has gotten my team on edge and why they brought Quinn in to help me." Robin laid his hand on Quinn's thigh.

Morgan eyed when they touched then said, "It doesn't bother you that Quinn's a double amputee? You're not a little weirded out that your new lover is missing his legs?"

"Morgan!" Quinn couldn't believe that Morgan would ask something like that. "You don't get to interrogate Robin like that."

Robin squeezed his leg. "Don't get angry at him, Quinn. He's just being your big brother. Morgan wants to make sure that I'll treat you right and see you as a whole person, not handicapped or crippled."

"I know you don't." Quinn wasn't going to let Morgan insult Robin though. "But I don't see why he needs to insult you like that—acting like you're only with me because you pity me."

Morgan shot him a quick glance. "I don't think he's with you because he pities you. Hell, Robin isn't that kind of guy. I'm pretty sure he doesn't do pity fucks."

Robin snorted. "God, that sounds terrible, doesn't it?"

"Actually I like the idea that you don't sleep with someone because you feel sorry for them. Not that I thought that's why you were sleeping with me or anything like that." He shook his head.

Robin was only half engaged in the current conversation, his head still spinning from the revelation that someone out there was airing his private business. Logically he knew that when you were as well-known as he was, it wasn't a matter of *if* someone pried into your life — it was when and under what circumstances.

He knew that until he spoke to Alfred and Coach Ramsey and at least set a time to meet with them, he'd be useless at any other sort of conversation.

Robin stood, surprising the other two with his sudden movement. "I have to make a phone call," he explained as he maneuvered around Quinn's chair then headed toward the bedrooms. After a moment of consideration, he went into the unused room and closed the door. It wasn't that he didn't want Quinn to hear anything — it was all going to be revealed eventually — he just couldn't look him in the eye until he'd made a move in the right direction.

When he opened his phone he noticed there was a missed call and a voicemail from Alfred. Grimacing, he turned the volume back up. He'd forgotten he'd turned it down at the interview then relied on the vibrate function for the text exchange with Quinn. He debated for a moment whether to listen or just call, then he succumbed to the inevitable and entered his passcode.

"Robin, it's Alfred. Give me a call when you're done with the interview and back at the hotel. Ramsey and I would like to get together and talk about something that's come up,

and that should probably happen tonight so you can concentrate on tennis tomorrow. We'll be at the hotel, so we can either meet in your suite or down in mine. I'll look for your call. Thanks."

Nothing to do but face the music now. He erased the voicemail, then dialed Alfred's line.

"Robin? How did the interview go?"

"Hi, Alfred." He knew he sounded dejected and tried to infuse a bit of strength into his voice. "It went well. I got your voicemail, and...I gathered from that asshole Justin's snide innuendos what it's about. I'd already decided I needed to talk to you guys—that's why I got my phone out and saw your voicemail. I mean, I'd turned down the volume—"

"Robin! Robin, take a breath. There's no need to panic. Let's talk about this in person, though. Do you want us to come up, or...?"

"Yes, that's fine. See you soon." Belatedly he remembered Morgan's presence, but then shrugged. The guy already seemed to know all about him anyway, and if Quinn trusted him, Robin would too.

He hung up and took a deep breath then another, trying to visualize Quinn's meditation techniques. Right now it wasn't working and he didn't want to hyperventilate, so he gave up and went back to the living room.

The combined gaze of the Damaris brothers on him as soon as he came back into view was almost enough to have him spinning in his tracks. A knock at the door just then announced the other men's arrival.

"Alfred and Coach," he explained, probably unnecessarily, as he detoured that direction to answer.

Both men wore their usual expressions until they'd entered far enough to see Morgan, who'd silently risen to stand next to and slightly in front of Quinn. Coach glanced thoughtfully between the two brothers, while Alfred narrowed his eyes.

"Robin, Quinn. We were hoping to have a private meeting—"

"It's okay," Robin interrupted as he led the men into the sitting area. "I don't mind Morgan being here."

Morgan and Quinn both looked a bit surprised and, Robin thought, pleased.

Ramsey took a seat after shaking hands and introducing himself to Morgan. Alfred was next, and his gaze had turned to calculating. "Good to meet you, Morgan. And just who are you to our Robin?"

Morgan's eyebrow shot up. "Well, I only met him for the first time today, but since he and my brother are...close, I'd like to think of him as slightly more than a friend."

Quinn coughed. Robin looked at him, but he was staring at Morgan with a warning expression.

He finally caught on and almost choked as well. Had Alfred thought that Morgan and Robin were...? But that would mean Alfred knew he liked men. How was that possible?

Though—he dropped onto the couch resignedly—if everyone knew about the drinking he did in the privacy of his bedroom, it probably wasn't a stretch to know what *else* he preferred to do in there if a person was determined to find out.

It wasn't nearly as scary anymore, for some reason, to think that his life was an open book to these men. Even when he'd been at his worst, they had stuck by him and seen the promise in him.

Time to put all his cards on the table and hope for the best.

Chapter Seventeen

"I guess we have a lot to talk about," Robin began. He tried to keep his gaze on Coach, since he was the hardest to read right then. But he kept finding himself glancing at Quinn, who watched him steadily.

"I'd like to start, please," he added to Alfred when he opened his mouth to say something. Alfred stopped and nodded for him to continue.

Even wanting to initiate the conversation and feeling the support from the men in the room, it was damned hard to make his mouth work around the words he needed to say. The silence built until Robin was nearly frantic with the need to break it.

"I'm gay," he blurted then winced.

Alfred and Coach looked patently unsurprised, though Quinn wore an interesting expression — somewhere between amusement and shock. He guessed that he hadn't been expecting to hear that thrown out to the group — even though he of course knew it was true — any more than Robin had planned for it to come out. "And I'm guessing by your lack of reaction that this isn't news to anyone."

Coach and Alfred exchanged a meaningful look, and Coach shook his head. "No, Robin. I had my suspicions before you came to Florida. Then when I saw how you reacted to Maximo..."

"Oh my God." Robin covered his face with his hands as it heated to flashpoint. The highly ranked American player Ramsey had also been coaching until Robin was twenty had been his first crush. It was humiliating to think that Coach, and possibly Max as well, had known of his interest.

"You followed him around like a puppy as a teenager, but then when you were older, well..." Coach cleared his throat. "Anyway, that's not what this is all about, and we don't need to know, unless of course you're messing around with someone on the Tour." He gave a small laugh at what he obviously considered to be an absurdity.

Note to self—never, ever let anyone know about Danie. Well, anyone else.

Robin attempted a small smile, unable to look at Quinn. "No, that's not what I wanted to say. I mean— I am, obviously since you knew already, but there's more..." God, he was butchering this.

"Robin—" Alfred began but he waved him silent, needing to excise it all.

Screwing up his courage, he told them, "I've been drinking. Not lately, but for a while there...yeah." He paused then forged ahead to the last piece. "And I'm still taking the Soma."

That revelation obviously took both Coach and Quinn by surprise. "What?" Coach frowned and turned to Alfred. "Did you know about this?"

Alfred sighed. "Rumors started up a couple of days ago. The drinking angle had feet since they could bring up his mother's death. But though the painkiller abuse story has come to light, it's just whispers at this point."

"It's not abuse!" Robin protested, looking automatically to Quinn, whose expression was blank as a mannequin's. "It's not. I just used it when my knee got a little sore. Well, and to help me sleep sometimes...but not lately at all. Not...now." Now that he and Quinn had been together. He silently pleaded with Quinn to believe him.

"Where have you been getting it? Because I know you didn't have any refills left on your prescription," Coach asked, his voice about as stern as Robin had ever heard it. "Not since the holidays last year, before the Australian."

Fuck. He hadn't thought about that part of it. Last thing he wanted was to throw Jerome under the bus. Robin jumped to his feet, unable to sit a moment longer. He opened his mouth then closed it again. "Hold on," he begged, his gaze darting between all of them, lingering on Quinn, who hadn't moved. "Fuck, just...hold on a sec. I'll be right back."

He hurried back to the same room he'd used to make the call earlier, hearing the murmur of voices behind him as they broke into a hushed conversation.

Robin dialed Jerome, not sure whether he wanted him to pick up or not.

"Hey," Jerome answered. "What's up? How'd your interview go?"

He sighed, dreading what was to come. "Fine. Listen, there's a lot of stuff going down right now. I'm talking to Coach and Alfred and, um..." Pacing back and forth didn't do his nerves any good so he sat on the edge of the bed. "I had to tell them about the pills."

"What?" Jerome screeched. "Oh fuck. Fuck, fuck, fuck. What...? Did it come out in the interview or something? Why would you *do* that?"

Robin cut in when Jerome took a breath. "I needed to come clean, because, yeah. Somehow the guy knew about it. Who else knows besides you?"

There was a tap on the door then it opened to reveal Quinn. Robin swallowed hard then motioned him inside. Quinn wheeled himself in and closed the door behind him.

Meanwhile, Jerome was freaking out. "No one! Well, besides the woman who works for me and her sister with the prescription, of course. But they wouldn't say anything. Why would they? Do they know about me? Are they pissed? Robin!"

"Shh, Jesus, quit screaming. No—not yet. They asked where it was coming from and I had to call you before I said anything."

Quinn's gaze sharpened on him and he tilted his head, obviously listening to whatever he could hear from both sides of the conversation.

"But, I have to tell them, Jerome." No point in hiding anything now.

Quinn's brow smoothed and he nodded slightly, as though in confirmation to himself of who he'd thought Robin was speaking with.

"Oh God. They're going to kill me. They're going to kill you." Jerome was having a complete meltdown.

"Stop it. You might as well come up to my suite. Everyone's up here and you're...involved as well."

"I was just trying to help you, you know. It's not fair that you're going to—"

"Stop right there. I know you thought you were helping, and I wouldn't betray you except for the fact that the whole truth needs to come out so we can all move on." He sounded like a self-help guru or something—laughable since he was the most messed-up one in the bunch.

Jerome let out a huge sigh that turned into a groan. "Fine. I know. Sorry. I'm just picturing my lackluster career going up in smoke as soon as Coach Ramsey finds out it was me. He's going to hate me."

"Come upstairs."

"Fine." Jerome hung up.

Robin put his phone back in his pocket, taking a bit more time than he needed before he raised his head to look at Quinn. "I'm sorry."

"I know," Quinn said then pressed his lips into a hard line, shook his head and sat back in his chair. "I had a suspicion about the drinking, actually. I told you right from the start that I can recognize the signs really well. And I knew you hadn't been drinking as much lately, which I was really happy about. But the painkillers—that was news to me, and it shouldn't have been."

God, he couldn't stop apologizing. "I'm sor—"

"I should have seen it. I think back now and can almost pick out the times when you'd taken it. When you'd been bouncing off the walls and suddenly you went so calm. I actually thought it was the alcohol. What? Vodka? It wasn't distinctive, whatever it was."

Robin grimaced. "Yeah. And I know it's a depressant, but it's always had sort of the opposite effect on me. Then I couldn't sleep…"

"And so you'd take the Soma. And Jerome was supplying it to you?"

"Ugh. Supplying sounds awful. It's not like it was illegal drugs or steroids or anything."

"It's illegal if you don't have a prescription." Quinn pinned him with his gaze for a few moments, then relented and held out his hand.

Robin went to his knees pathetically fast at the opening. "I'm so sorry."

"You don't need to apologize to me."

"Yes, I do." There was some noise from out in the other room.

When Robin stood and went to open the door, he heard Coach's voice. "I'm sorry, Jerome. It's not a good time—"

"Robin called me and told me to come up," Jerome interjected, slipping past Ramsey into the room as Robin and Quinn came back into the sitting area. "Hey."

"Hey. Thanks for coming up."

Robin warily looked from Jerome to their coach, and it was obvious he had made the connection. He went completely still and reddened, glaring at Jerome. Jerome started to shake his head and Coach held up a hand.

"Are you using them too?"

"No!" Jerome denied. "No, I—"

"Do you realize the jeopardy you've put not only your career in, but Robin's? And not just his *career*, either. You do know what happened to his mother. I've spent the last decade trying to keep him away from the same fate and you delivered drugs to him like..." Coach trailed off as though he couldn't come up with an analogy bad enough. Or maybe he'd seen Robin go still at the mention of his mother and his concern for Robin, and how long he'd been carrying that responsibility.

And he'd thought he couldn't feel any worse.

"I think at this point, you all need to do less playing the blame game and more deciding how to mitigate the damage."

Everyone startled when Morgan spoke up. Robin had almost forgotten he was in the room. Jerome was probably wondering who the hell he was. A short burst of hysterical laughter escaped, and as though choreographed, everyone turned from Morgan to him, which made him laugh harder.

"I'm sorry," he managed. "It's not funny at all, I know. I don't know why I'm laughing."

It did something to break the tension and bring the room down from high alert. Robin walked over past Jerome, getting a clap on the shoulder from him as he passed, then he faced Coach Ramsey. "I am sorry I put us all in this situation."

"It's not your fault, at least not entirely. Everyone in this room with the exception of the Damaris boys had a part in some way." Coach held his arms open, his lips pressed tight. "Come here, son."

Robin dove against the usually stoic man who had been a second surrogate father to him since he was a boy. He blinked hard to try to keep the emotions at bay, but it was a losing battle.

Coach only held him for a few moments then firmly put him away at arm's length. "Now sit. Alfred has some things we need to decide as a group. You too, Jerome."

Jerome froze then reversed his stealthy progress he'd been making toward the door.

Robin began to automatically head toward Quinn then paused, uncertain. It probably wasn't good to assume that Quinn would be willing to give him a shoulder to lean on.

Like always, his eyes found their way to Quinn. Relief soared as Quinn held out a hand and took Robin's as soon as he was close enough to reach. He worked their positions around until Robin was seated on the couch beside Morgan and Quinn was parked next to him, their knees touching at an angle.

The warmth of that small contact and his hand in Quinn's was more than enough to settle the last of his worries. They would have to move forward from this setback, but Quinn wasn't going to let him drown alone in his mistakes.

"We need to discuss our strategy for handling this in the press," Alfred began. "I think striking first and releasing the information the way we want it will have the best outcome. We also need to hire someone to find out who it was that brought this out and what their goals are—"

"No need," Morgan interrupted. He stood. "You— I'll need to talk to." He pointed to Jerome then crooked his finger. Jerome looked ill as he hesitantly rose. "In the other room, while they discuss damage control. I need names and details to get started." He walked away without another word. Jerome shot Robin a wide-eyed look then followed.

Everyone watched them leave the room then glanced at Quinn, who shrugged. "It's sort of his thing. He'll be able to get the information faster and cheaper than anyone you could ever hire. You can trust him to keep it quiet."

Alfred nodded. "That's fine then." He opened a screen on his tablet. "Let's get started on a press release. I want to get this out before your match so it will stop the bad press in its tracks."

Chapter Eighteen

After their long flight to Australia from Switzerland, Quinn had stayed in Melbourne to stock the rental house and settle in, while Robin had opted to continue on to Sydney to watch Jerome in the Apia International tournament men's doubles final tomorrow. It was strange being alone in a hotel room tonight after so much time with Quinn, especially after the holiday break in the Tour from November to January where they'd basically stayed at home, trained, made love and generally enjoyed a honeymoon period after their busy life following the US Open.

Robin's simple public acknowledgment that he'd previously misused prescription painkillers and alcohol, but was working hard on the road back to health, had been met by a few loud-mouths embarrassing themselves in a quiet room. All the sensationalism had been removed by their preemptive announcement, and with other sports figures in the news for much worse, it wasn't more than days until even the worst of the media had moved on, especially after no further revelations were forthcoming. Some less savory pundits had initially implied that admitting to the painkillers was a cover for worse—up to and including meth and steroids. But every supposedly 'random' drug test Robin submitted to came up clean, and there wasn't much arguing anyone could do with that.

Danie and several other players had been publicly vocal in their support of Robin's honesty and character, and had rallied around him, especially at the Open when everything had first come out. The US Open had ended up being Robin's strongest showing of the year to that point, and he'd advanced to the semis before losing to the eventual champion.

It was what had happened afterwards that had taken them all by surprise. Offers for interviews, not with investigative journalists or even sports media, but with news shows, late night hosts and mainstream magazines had started pouring in. Evidently Robin had struck a chord with his history, his fallibility, the fall then rise back to the top. Everyone wanted to talk to him or put him on a cover to Alfred's surprise and delight. It had been more than a little overwhelming and had forced Robin to discuss many parts of his life he'd have been more comfortable keeping to himself—his mother's very public alcoholism and addictions, leading to her eventual death, the lack of knowledge of who his father was, and more recently, the cold shoulder he'd received from his mom and dad—aunt and uncle he supposed they were now—who had turned on him after the announcement.

His aunt wouldn't even speak to him. His uncle had broken their silence once to briefly explain that she couldn't bear to deal with another downward spiral, thinking it was inevitable that he'd follow his mother's path, and had told him to respect their wishes not to contact them again. The lack of faith in him had been both disheartening but somewhat expected.

Robin still hoped that at some point they'd realize he wasn't going to break their hearts like his mother had, and they could reconcile. After all, they were all the family he had. Blood family, anyway.

Morgan had found that gossip, sex and greed had led to the information about Robin's private life getting out. Anke, his housekeeper, had been at a bridal shower for a friend and had gotten to talking to Jerome's housekeeper — the same one whose sister had gotten the Soma from her physician for Jerome. After a few drinks, Anke shared the tidbit about how many vodka bottles she cleaned out of Robin's home on a weekly basis, and Jerome's maid had taken that information and run with it.

Evidently she wanted to be more than Jerome's employee, and blamed Robin for taking up so much of Jerome's time — that, and she took to heart his good-natured griping about how if he used the time he spent training with Robin to develop his own game, he'd finally break into the top fifty. So she'd contacted a few tabloids to see if they would buy her story on Robin's drug and alcohol use, which had started the rumors just before the US Open.

It had backfired on her in a big way. Jerome, of course, had gone ballistic when Morgan had told him about it. Robin had been less upset and more hurt. He'd truly liked Anke, but he obviously couldn't keep her on after she'd so blatantly, if innocently, violated her confidentiality agreement. The day after she'd been terminated, Margerite had brought her niece Francoise in and had point-blank asked Robin to hire her rather than have her interview applicants to fill the position.

Robin hadn't spent much time at home, though. He was back to full-time play on the Tour, so trips home were few and far between. Quinn had been along every step of the way.

He got up and crossed the room to the ice bucket before he realized what he was doing. Stopping short with one hand on the container, it was as though he'd gotten a face full of its contents. Alone in a hotel room for the first time in ages, and what had he automatically done? The first step he'd need for a glass of vodka rocks. God, was this what he was headed for any time he was alone?

Shaken, Robin retreated to the bed and sat down. He picked up his cell phone and dialed.

"Robbie?"

Strike two. Not sure why he'd called Danie instead of Quinn or even Jerome, he didn't answer Danie right away.

"Hey, what's wrong? Robbie? You there?"

He almost hung up but that was stupid when Danie knew it was him. "Hi Danie."

"There you are. Thought I'd lost ya. You in Melbourne already?"

"Not yet. Sydney."

Danie paused as if thinking. "You aren't playing at Apia..."

"No, just stopped over to watch Jerome tomorrow. He and Cal are in the men's doubles final."

"Ah, gotcha." There was a rustling sound, and Robin had a mental image of Danie stretching out in bed. "Well, obviously this isn't a booty call since you know I'm not in the city, so what's on your mind, *brah*? Come on—talk to Papa Coetzee."

"Oh God, do not call yourself Papa. That's just wrong."

Danie's chuckle helped him relax even further. Their relationship had taken a definite turn after Wimbledon, the last time they'd been together in any way more than fraternal. Once they'd taken the strange dynamics of sex out of the equation, they'd forged a stronger friendship—though they would always have a competitive edge to it, at least until they were both retired someday way down the line.

"Just weird being alone in a hotel room. Haven't been since the French." Then he confessed the real issue, "I about started fixing a drink just now."

"Robbie—" Danie started, his tone dead serious.

"Not literally. Don't worry. I don't even have any alcohol here and don't plan to get any, either. Just started getting ice on autopilot and it sort of hit me."

"Well I'm glad you called me, although I'm a bit surprised you're alone. Where's your American watchdog?"

"He went ahead to Melbourne. To get the house stocked for next week. No reason for him to hang out here to watch Jerome play. I mean…"

Danie remained silent.

"Fine," Robin caved. Danie knew him too well. "I changed my plans at the last minute. I needed…a little space, I guess."

"He pressuring you for more than you want?"

"No." More like the opposite. "I can't get attached," he admitted. "To him, I'm a job…with perks. But a job nonetheless. He's gonna leave in six months or whatever when his contract is up and…" And it was going to break Robin's heart to watch him go. Better to maintain a buffer if he could. Keep it light. Prove occasionally—like tonight—that he didn't *need* Quinn, so when the time came, he could pick himself up and move on.

"It'll be okay. Things have a way of working out."

"Nice platitude."

"You're welcome."

Robin's phone chimed with an incoming call. Quinn. His heart leapt—stupid thing. Almost as dumb as his cock, which was suddenly all in favor of some phone sex.

"I have a call, so…"

"No worries. Sleep well. I'll see you in a couple days."

"Yeah, good night. And thanks." Robin switched lines. "Hello?"

"Hi. I was sure I was going to go to voicemail. I didn't wake you, did I?" Quinn's voice in his ear sent a shiver through him that Danie's never had.

"No, I was just on the phone."

"Oh." There was a long, awkward pause that Robin struggled not to fill then Quinn finally asked, "Jerome?"

"No. Danie." He quickly moved on. "So how's the house?" They'd rented one that Danie had used a few times for the Open in the past since it had a private tennis court and a tall privacy wall, as well as a covered pool. But the reason he'd thought it better suited for Robin to use this year was that it was actually wheelchair accessible. So he'd had his agent give Alfred the information and had found another house to use this year. "Pretty nice, huh?" Robin continued when Quinn didn't answer right away.

"Yeah. It's nice." Quinn's flat tone was a long way removed from the reaction Robin had been expecting now that Quinn had seen the place.

"What's wrong?"

"Nothing. Just wanted to say goodnight and remind you to avoid too much junk at the tournament tomorrow."

Yeah right. He could let it go and pretend he believed Quinn, but his mouth had different ideas. "Bullshit. Obviously something is bothering you, so why don't you just say it? Is it because I was talking to Danie on the phone? That's a bit immature to get jealous if I talk to another man." Robin knew he sounded like an ass but it pissed him off that Quinn would pull such a lie.

Nothing wrong, my ass.

Something was wrong for him to get that tone of voice and short on words.

"That's not why I'm jealous." Quinn's admission lingered over the phone line for a few moments.

"Okay...so what is it you're jealous of? Danie isn't even in Sydney, so it's not as though we're secretly hooking up behind your back. Are you upset at me having a friend besides you? That's ridiculous. Or—"

"You fucked him in this house, didn't you?"

Robin was shocked speechless by Quinn's harsh, uncensored question. *Oh fuck.* If he'd thought Quinn sounded jealous before, he'd been mistaken. His voice was saturated with it now. He mentally scrambled for an answer that wouldn't escalate the situation.

"Have you ever slept with someone in your bed in Colorado?"

"What?"

"You heard the question. Answer me. Have you fucked someone in your bed at home?"

Quinn slowly answered, "Yes."

"Should I be jealous of that if I ever went to Colorado to be with you there?"

"But that was before we'd even...met..." Quinn trailed off.

Bingo. "You seeing my point?"

Quinn sighed, sounding a lot more like himself at last. "Doesn't mean I have to like it."

"It's a great house, and we'll be staying there together. Can't you put your imagination to better use and maybe come up with ideas on what we can do together, especially before Coach and Jerome get back?" They were staying in Sydney for a few more nights before coming to Melbourne—Jerome so he could see the sights, and their coach so he could visit with an old friend.

Quinn closed his eyes and took a deep breath. *Jesus!* When had he ever been jealous of a boyfriend? *Never.* Yet the moment he'd heard Robin say he'd been talking to Danie, Quinn had wanted to demand to know everything they'd said.

Robin was right. As far as Quinn knew, everything that had happened between Robin and the Afrikaner had been before Quinn and he had gotten together. Him being jealous was just as silly as Robin being jealous of all the men Quinn had fucked.

"It's actually a really nice house and you'll have to thank Coetzee for recommending it for us. I don't have any problem with my chair or too many stairs." He scrubbed his hand over his face. *Get your head out of your ass, Damaris.* "I think I can come up with a few ideas."

"Yeah? Like what?"

It was almost as though Robin was daring him. He grinned and cleared his throat. "Oh, are you naked right now?"

Robin coughed. "Are we going to have phone sex?"

"Maybe. I just thought I'd ask what you're wearing, because I like to think of you lying on your hotel bed, naked and touching yourself while I talk to you."

He heard rustling over the phone as though Robin was removing his clothes. Quinn was already lying on his bed in just a pair of sweats. He reached down to wrap his hand around his cock then stroked it.

"Robin," he moaned.

"What? I'm here. Are you jerking off?"

"Yeah." He closed his eyes. "I'm thinking about you straddling my hips and stretching your ass. I never thought it was a kink of mine, but apparently you getting yourself ready for me to fuck turns me on."

Robin grunted. "I love you watching me while I do it. Knowing that your fat cock is going to be filling me gets me hard and dripping."

Quinn bit his lip as he remembered how tight and hot Robin had been the last time they'd made love. How Robin had used his mouth to roll the condom on Quinn before giving him a blowjob that had taken him right to the edge.

"I'm thinking about how you grab my dick in your hand and position me perfectly so you can just slide down, impaling yourself. You don't stop until I'm buried balls-deep in you."

They both moaned and Quinn stopped for a moment, getting lube from the nightstand to squirt into his palm. Coating his shaft eased the friction a little, letting him pump faster. He gritted his teeth, holding his climax at bay.

"Once you let me know you're all right, I grab your hips hard enough to leave bruises then lift you off me until only the tip of my cock is inside you. Then I slam you back down, doing my best to nail your gland with each thrust."

"Uh…" Robin didn't sound as though he was capable of talking at that moment and Quinn used that as encouragement.

"I fuck you harder and harder while you jerk yourself off. The combination of my dick and your hand is driving you closer and closer. The pleasure is building, Robin. You love how I'm rough with you. You were made to take my cock like you do." He swallowed back saying that Robin was perfect for him in every way because they had never discussed what was going on between them. It had mostly been sex or helping Robin get his head on straight to get back in the game.

"God yes," Robin said. "No one's ever fucked me like you. I can always feel you for a day or two afterward. I love that."

Quinn could hear the need and want in Robin's voice, and along with the way his own balls were drawing tight to his body, he was close.

"I want you to come right now, Robin. Spill your cum all over your hand and stomach."

"Quinn!" Robin shouted then the phone line was filled with pants and whimpers as Robin must have come when Quinn told him to.

He didn't wait until Robin's climax had eased before he came. With a yell, Quinn let go of his control and coated his own body with cum. He shuddered for a little while as his nerves began to ease from the overload of pleasure.

"Robin, are you all right?" he asked once he'd caught his breath.

"Yes," Robin panted. "Just trying not to pass out on you."

He chuckled before saying, "That's fine, man. Go to bed. We can talk tomorrow."

"Can't wait to get to Melbourne and see what else you have in mind for us." Robin laughed.

"Oh I'll come up with some more ways we can try out this comfortable bed by the time you get here." Quinn took a deep breath. "I'm sorry about how I acted earlier. I was jealous, but you're right. Whatever we each did before we got together isn't important. What's important is what we're doing right now."

"Thanks, Quinn." Robin sounded sleepy.

Quinn smiled. "Sweet dreams, Robin. I know I'll be having them."

Robin said goodnight, and Quinn hung up. He tossed the phone onto the table then climbed back into his chair. *Might as well go take a quick shower or I'll wake up stuck to the sheets.* He grinned as he headed to the bathroom, eagerly looking forward to when Robin would arrive in Melbourne and they could have a little more fun in bed.

Chapter Nineteen

"Advantage, Keller."

Break point. He hadn't seen many today. It had been a ridiculously tight game, so he really needed to capitalize and not let it get back to deuce. He had to break Ping's serve, right now. He'd won the tiebreaks in the first two sets, but they'd been hard fought. He'd just as soon put this set away on serve after a service break.

Robin focused in on his opponent across the net. Ping had a very fast service motion, almost abbreviated, so if you weren't paying attention, it would come at you a moment sooner than you expected. Of course, sacrificing height on the toss also meant he came in with a lot of spin as opposed to power, which was fine with Robin.

Sure enough the toss was short and Ping kicked the serve out to his forehand. Robin was in great position and sent it back down the line. Ping got there—he was fast—but didn't have enough arm to get it over the net.

"Game, Keller. Five games to four, third set."

God, it never got old, getting to what would hopefully be the last game of an important match — one that would put him into the semi-finals of a Grand Slam.

Before he took his place on the service line, he flicked a quick glance at the player's box where Ramsey, Jerome and Quinn were seated. Like everyone around them, their entire focus was on him. He couldn't make out their eyes, but he imagined Quinn's warm gaze.

His first serve was an ace, and he celebrated inside, though he didn't let it show.

"Fifteen-love."

His first serve percentage from the deuce court had been a bit lower than usual, so he took a bit off, but that allowed Ping to grab control of the return. After several exchanges, he had been worked way over to his backhand side, so when Ping sent a perfectly placed drop shot to his forehand, he knew right away he wouldn't get there.

"Fifteen all."

After wiping his hands and face off, he tossed the towel back to a ball boy then accepted three balls, choosing the best two. He rocked back and tossed the ball then brought the racquet around. Another ace down the mid-court line.

"Thirty-fifteen."

He went through the toweling off process again then got another ball. Remembering what had happened when he'd tried to baby his weak side serve, he rocketed this one out wide and Ping sent the return way out past the baseline.

"Forty-fifteen. Double match point, Keller."

Robin blew out a breath and took his time choosing between three balls, hitting one back to the ball boy, pocketing another and pinning his hopes on the third.

C'mon. C'mon.

He sent the ball skyward and even though his toss was a little off, he adjusted and put it into play. Ping was playing for his life—nothing to lose at this point—and he hit a hard return crosscourt to Robin's forehand. Robin went down the line to Ping's backhand…

"Game, set, match, Keller."

Robin whooped with joy, pounded the extra ball into the stands, then jogged to the net to shake with Ping. Applause filled the Rod Laver Arena, drowning out the chair umpire as he recounted the scores of each set. Robin took his turn shaking with the umpire then headed to his bags, ecstatic to be advancing to the semis. As usual he exchanged his game racquet for the autographed giveaway, which he left out, then stuffed the rest of his belongings into his two bags and closed them up.

His team was still on their feet watching him, including Quinn, so he waved in their direction and his grin widened even further when Quinn sent him a wink.

As he walked to the exit from the court, he handed the racquet to a young boy with a missing tooth and a huge grin, then paused to take a pen and sign a few things that were being thrust his way. Even though he wanted to get to Quinn, he forced himself to take his time and interact with the fans for about a minute before he followed Ping off the court. There was no rush. He was going to have time to clean up and change into his off-court clothes before meeting Quinn, especially since they would have to navigate the arena and the crowds to get to the players' entrance where they'd arranged to meet.

Yes, he was riding high.

* * * *

Two days later, he was trying to recall that fantastic feeling. There was no shame in losing in the semis...

Again, his mind helpfully added. That was two Grand Slams in a row where he'd gotten to the semis relatively easily, but hadn't made the finals.

They'd been heading back to the house when Danie had called to see what he was doing. His hitting partner had lost in an early round and gone home right after, and Danie's coach was newly married, so his wife and he were out at dinner together. It occurred to Robin that Danie wasn't really close to any of the guys on the Tour. He had somewhat of a rep of being an iceman, though Robin knew he was a big softie underneath. After all the times Danie had been there for him, Robin couldn't let him sit around alone the night before a big match, even though he wasn't sure he'd be great company.

"You sure it's okay if I pop over? I can just—"

"Of course you can. As long as it's not too late for you." Danie's semi-final match was the next day.

"I probably won't be there long. Just need a bit of company because I'm going out of my head. I need to grab something to eat on the way over, though."

"Tell him we have food," Quinn interjected, obviously able to overhear Danie's voice from his position next to Robin in the back seat.

Robin turned to Quinn. "*Are you sure?*" he mouthed.

Quinn nodded, so Robin had to take him at face value, even though he was a bit leery about having his current partner cooking for someone from his past. "We have plenty of food, Quinn says, and trust me — it's way better tasting and better for you than anything you could pick up."

"I don't want to be a bother."

"No bother," Quinn spoke loud enough to hear. "I planned ahead and fixed plenty of food to be easy to grab and put out after we got back from the match tonight."

"There you have it then. Come on over — we'll be there soon." They said their goodbyes and hung up. Belatedly Robin realized he should have probably asked Jerome and Coach, who were engrossed in a conversation about another double team, if it was okay too.

I'm a rude bastard.

When they got to the house, Danie was already there waiting out in front of the gate. His rental was only a few blocks away, so he must have walked. Once the driver keyed in the code, Danie walked through the opening gate and continued up the drive to wait by the side door.

"Thanks for the invite," Danie greeted him and gave him a side hug. Then he shook hands with Ramsey and Jerome before turning to Quinn. "And thank you for offering up some supper."

Quinn nodded but didn't linger. He probably wanted to get his prosthetics off.

Inside they all broke for their separate rooms except for Robin and Danie. Danie led the way into the kitchen. "Thirsty?" he asked as he opened the fridge.

"Yes, very, but don't let Quinn catch you acting the host in our damn house," he warned as he accepted a bottle of water.

"My bad. Just habit, you know? You live in a place a few times and it sort of becomes yours."

They went to go sit outside on the patio in the evening air, and Robin found himself venting about the match to Danie in a way that would have been hard with the others. Coach would analyze every shot to death, Jerome would be blindly loyal and tell him over and over how he'd been robbed, and Quinn—he never really discussed Robin's game. He'd said once that since he only had a layman's knowledge of the game, it really wasn't his place to give opinions, though he would answer questions honestly if asked. Most of the time it was a relief to hang out with Quinn after a match since they always had things outside of tennis to discuss, but once in a while, it was good to decompress and talk about the game with someone who knew not only tennis in general, but the Tour, his opponent...hell, even Robin himself intimately.

His game, that was.

The sun was long gone but its warmth lingered. It had been ridiculously hot today on the court. He said as much to Danie, adding, "Don't keel over with heatstroke or anything tomorrow."

"I'm ready for it, so don't worry about me."

"Yeah, well, I sort of like you a little. It would suck having to find someone else who can keep up with me while I work through my frustration after a loss."

A snort came from behind them, and they turned to see Quinn coming their way in his chair. "Good thing I know what you meant by that."

Robin tried to think back to what he'd said. "Huh?"

"Never mind. I put out the food buffet style if you guys want to come fix your plates. I'd get in there fast. Jerome looked hungry."

Quinn seemed much more relaxed than Robin had expected, given his past reactions to Danie. Danie walked inside and Robin hung back with Quinn.

"Thanks for including Danie."

"He's your friend, and you need more than just me and Coach in your life."

"Don't forget Jerome," Robin joked as they approached the door.

"How could I? He wouldn't let us."

Quinn and Robin laughed together. Quinn grinned up at Robin, then he suddenly stopped his progress and Robin paused too, trying to figure out why. "You okay?"

"Yes, I'm good." Quinn looked up at Robin with a hungry gaze that had Robin swallowing hard. "And when everyone leaves or goes to bed, I'll prove it to you."

Robin couldn't wait.

Chapter Twenty

"Robin."

His eyes opened at the sound of his name. He'd been combining post-travel stretching with Quinn's meditation techniques and had sort of drifted away. "Hey there."

"Hey yourself. Sorry to pull you out of the zone, but I want to keep you on track for dinner so that you still have time for a snack before bed."

Robin knew Quinn's feeling on eating at regular intervals on the ramp up to a tournament. It was probably a good thing as his appetite could be unreliable. He'd had horrible eating habits before Quinn had come into his life. Even now, he made himself eat more by the clock than his internal prompting, because as long as he stayed hydrated, he rarely got hungry until it was too late.

"Okay. Do I have time to clean up?"

"Sure, but don't linger. I made a frittata so it's better warm. Speaking of which, I need to go check on it so it doesn't turn into charcoal under the broiler." Quinn was already moving back in the direction of the kitchen in his chair. He generally split his days between his legs and his chair while they were at home.

Don't forget – this isn't his home.

Just like that, all of his relaxation fled, along with – to a lesser extent – his excitement from winning the warm-up tournament yesterday. Robin sighed. Might as well take his shower.

As he rinsed off, he considered how the best period of his life so far had had a corresponding gray edge. His career was back on track, but the speed of the calendar moving toward the French – and end of Quinn's contract – had been relentless. Even since the Australian, Robin and Quinn had been traveling almost nonstop to tournaments as Robin fought to raise his ATP ranking and pull in some prize money. Not that he was having financial difficulties or anything, but the big dip his earnings had taken last year had been a huge eye opener.

He really had a limited time in which to earn his living for the rest of his life, and no idea what else he might do after his career was over. And it wasn't like he had a high success rate when it came to making good decisions. All the best moves in his life had been initiated by someone else, it seemed.

He'd missed seeing Quinn after the final in Madrid yesterday. He'd flown back right after he'd finished watching Robin's match, while Robin had been tapped for interviews all that evening then a photo shoot for a sponsor's ad campaign early today. It hadn't really made sense for Quinn to hang around, and that was partially why Robin had been so fixated on what would happen after Quinn's time was done. Yesterday was just a taste – no one to celebrate with after the match, or to curl up against in the hotel room. No one next to him on the flight home.

At least he hadn't been tempted to drink. That was a relief, though Robin wasn't stupid enough to think that it might not become a temptation again. Once an alcoholic, always an alcoholic. Jerome was convinced that he wasn't one, but with his mother's issues, Robin wasn't taking any chances by dismissing the possibility. As far as he was concerned, he would own that label and use it to keep himself from slipping back into bad habits.

Robin dried off then got dressed in something easy to take off. It had been tempting to tackle Quinn to the floor as soon as he'd gotten home from his flight earlier, but with Margerite and Francoise in the house, he'd been forced to keep their greeting quiet and a promise for later. Then he'd decided to work through his frustration and adrenaline with some meditation, and to his surprise, it had been somewhat successful...at least, as long as he didn't think about Quinn and riding his huge...

Damn it.

Robin looked ruefully down at his semi-hard shaft, obvious against his sweatpants, then shrugged. Oh well. The women were gone now, so no reason to be modest.

He enjoyed Quinn's reaction when he came around the corner, his interested gaze running the length of him. "Looks like you're ready...for dinner."

"Ha-ha." Robin hovered for a moment. "Anything I can help with?"

"Just the drinks." Quinn pointed to a pitcher of some kind of iced tea, on a tray with two glasses of ice.

Robin brought it over to the table and took a seat. "This looks great. Is that arugula from the kitchen garden bed?" He'd listened to Quinn rhapsodize on about how wonderful it was to have fresh herbs and greens over and over until he'd added a wheelchair-height raised bed to the sunny area off the side patio by the kitchen as a surprise this spring. Quinn had been shocked and pleased and had promptly started planning what to plant. Robin found he'd enjoyed surprising Quinn with renovations and additions to make his life easier and his stay in his home more enjoyable. And it wasn't as though Robin didn't benefit from it.

"Mmm hmm." Quinn hummed his assent around a bite of his frittata. "The chives too. I love having that there. I always wanted a garden, but I'm never home long enough for it to be practical. I'd either miss planting things on time or not be there when they're ready to harvest."

Robin warmed from the inside out at Quinn's enthusiasm. He was becoming somewhat addicted to pleasing him.

"I'm going to miss it when I leave," Quinn added and the glow was snuffed out.

Robin lowered his head and applied himself to eating the meal he no longer had much of an appetite for, as good as it was. The sooner they got done eating, the sooner they could go to bed and reconnect.

"You were hungry. What did you eat today?"

Wincing, Robin kept his eyes averted. "Not much. But I had that shoot, then the flight home and you don't want me to eat the stuff at airports..."

"Robin..."

"I know, I know." He finally met Quinn's eyes and gestured with his fork to his almost empty plate. "See, I'm eating healthy now. You're good for me."

The emotions that rose must have been evident in his eyes. Quinn put his fork down and reached out to him. "Come here."

Robin took his hand and leaned over to take a long, deep kiss. Quinn slid his hand down along his cock, which had been at least semi-hard since his shower. One layer of fabric between that point of contact was a huge tease, so Robin pulled back from the kiss to undo the tie of his pants, shove them down and step out of them before kicking them under the table.

He smiled in invitation then turned around and headed toward Quinn's suite, wearing only his shirt. Quinn's laugh followed him from the room as he put a little extra body language into his hips.

By the time Quinn joined him, he'd discarded his shirt and found the lube. He crawled over to the far side of the bed to give Quinn room to transfer from his chair to the mattress, then lay down and began to give himself a coat of lube inside and out.

"Stretch yourself," Quinn ordered but Robin shook his head.

"I already did enough stretching today."

"Not that kind." He pulled off his shirt and the movement of muscles in his torso, as always, drew Robin's admiring gaze and his free hand. He ran his touch down Quinn's arm, then across his chest when he lay down to shuck off his pants. He too had gone commando.

"Mmm. Love a man who's ready to go." Robin sat up and swung his leg over Quinn to straddle him.

"Well, I know how you are when you come off a tournament." Quinn's voice was a little strained as Robin slid along his hard cock, dragging his balls along it and painting Quinn's abs with a few drops of clear pre-cum.

Robin leaned over to grab a condom and tossed it onto Quinn's chest. "How's that?" he asked as he backed off enough to let Quinn roll the condom on.

"Needing." Quinn rocked his hips and Robin knee-walked back up into position then leaned down against Quinn's chest as he thrust between his ass cheeks, glancing over his hole.

A bit more lube and Robin held Quinn's cock upright behind him as he lowered himself. The initial twinge of penetration was as sweet as ever, and Robin paused to savor it as long as he could until Quinn gripped his hips and began to fuck up into him in short little bursts.

Robin let Quinn take control and lightly rode his movements, tugging on his own erection. When Quinn lifted him off his cock, Robin groaned in protest.

"Shh. Roll over."

Robin smiled to himself as he lay down on his stomach, spreading his legs apart to accommodate Quinn as he moved between them. He didn't waste any time in reentering Robin and the new angle took his breath away.

"God, this is..." Quinn didn't finish his thought but leaned down until his chest was resting on Robin's back. He ran his forearms under Robin to brace some of his weight and pressed down until Robin was completely covered by Quinn. Surrounded by him, helpless to do anything but accept him.

Quinn used only his hips to keep the slow rhythm of thrusts regular until Robin was going insane from the deliberate pace. He tried to move his arm to reach his cock but Quinn's arms made it impossible.

"You need more?"

"Need something. You're killing me. Fuck me like you mean it."

"Oh, I mean it." Quinn gave a couple of hard thrusts that made Robin gasp, then paused. "Like that?"

"Yeah. Oh fuck…"

Quinn picked up the pace and propped himself up into a push-up. The new angle and his hand to thrust into brought Robin to his peak almost instantly.

He groaned as he came into his hand and all over the mattress underneath him. Quinn placed the flat of his hand under Robin's pelvis then pulled up just a bit as he finished in a volley of thrusts that felt almost good enough to have Robin coming again.

Robin didn't move a muscle as Quinn caught his breath then slowly withdrew and moved away. He was aware of Quinn getting into his chair and probably heading to the bathroom, but couldn't seem to open his eyes as he breathed in the scent of Quinn from his pillow.

Chapter Twenty-One

The next thing Robin knew he opened his eyes and it was completely dark. After a quick, disoriented glance around confirmed he was home and in Quinn's room, he relaxed again and noticed Quinn lying next to him.

He turned over to lie facing him and realized he wasn't sleeping.

"Can't sleep?" he whispered.

Quinn heaved a huge sigh that made Robin's chest go tight. The tone of it told Robin that something was very wrong. He began to sit up and reach for the bedside light, but Quinn grabbed his arm. "Don't. It's okay. Just come here."

"Tell me what's wrong," Robin insisted as he acquiesced and snuggled against Quinn's lightly haired chest, trying hard to relax.

The silence dragged on a beat too long for comfort and just when Robin was about to burst with his impatience, Quinn finally said, "I'm leaving tomorrow."

Robin frowned. "Oh. Where are you going?"

"To see Morgan."

His heart began to pound as it started to sink in what Quinn was saying. "For how long?"

"You know the answer to that. It's time, Robin. You don't need me anymore."

Robin sat up despite Quinn's effort to keep him at his side. "No. Don't leave. You can't." He seized upon the first excuse he could. "We have a contract. You're supposed to be here for a year. You can't break the contract."

"Are you really going to use the contract to keep me here if I want to go?"

Oh God. Quinn *wanted* to go—wanted to leave Robin. He was speechless and it was hard to suck in air, as though he'd taken a blow to the solar plexus.

"Shh. Breathe," Quinn began to soothe him, but Robin wanted nothing of it.

"How can I...?" He tried again. "Fine. If you want to go, you're going to go. There's obviously not much I can do about that." He swung his legs over the side of the bed and stood.

"Robin, don't leave like—"

"Ha!" he spit out with a short, harsh laugh. "That's a good one. 'Don't leave'. You get to use that on me when you won't let me use it on you? Not fucking likely."

Suddenly all the strength left his legs. He'd known this was coming, but he'd never imagined Quinn would leave him before the contract ended—never imagined he'd hit him with this blindside. He sat heavily onto the edge of the mattress again and couldn't even force himself to move when Quinn ran his hand down his back.

"You'll be fine. You've come so far and I'm so proud—"

"Please don't use the stupid motivational pep talk crap on me you use with all your clients. Though, I guess that's all I am—a client." Robin barely recognized his voice.

"This was always more than a client relationship, and you know it. That's why I'm leaving now and not when the contract tells me to."

Robin couldn't make sense of any of it.

"Come back to bed."

Robin had a dozen blistering replies to that burning his throat, but in the time it took to settle on any one of them, his body had betrayed him and he'd lain back down.

"You'll do just fine."

"Don't fucking talk to me. One more word about how fine I'll be and I'm going upstairs."

Quinn fell silent and lay down on his own pillow. Robin listened to the familiar sound of his breathing for a very, very long time where neither of them spoke, and neither of them slept.

* * * *

Stuffing the last pile of his shirts into one of his suitcases, Quinn frowned. He hated the idea of leaving Robin, but it was time. He'd done all he could to help Robin get back on track and with the amount of matches won increasing, he saw that his job was done. Robin now had all the tools he needed to keep his career successful.

God, he didn't want to leave. He'd come to really care about Robin, not just as a client, but as a friend and lover as well. Yet Robin hadn't asked him to stay, so there was no reason to assume he would.

Robin had been training like crazy for the French Open. In fact he was out on the court right now, hitting balls with Jerome. He'd just returned from winning one of the warm-up tournaments and his excitement had translated into some amazing sex the night before.

He spun his chair around to head back to the dresser to grab his last bunch of briefs. Quinn had taught Margerite how to make a lot of the recipes he'd put into Robin's diet and she'd excelled at making them. That way Robin wouldn't have to hire a chef if he didn't want to.

Sighing, he tossed the underwear into the case before zipping it closed. He rested his forehead on the edge of the luggage and closed his eyes. He always hated this part of the job. While none of his former clients had come to mean as much to him as Robin had, he had been sad about saying goodbye to them. Yet he'd looked forward to his next job—wherever it took him.

Quinn rubbed his knees where they ached. He set the luggage by his door then left to head to the kitchen. Margerite glanced up as he entered. She smiled at him.

"How are you, Mr Damaris?"

His French had gotten much better over the year he'd spent with Robin, so he understood what she'd asked. "I'm doing well, Margerite. Have you called for a car?"

"Yes, sir."

He could tell she wanted to ask something, but she was too polite to do so. "I see you have Robin's snack ready. I'll take it out to him."

"Certainly." She placed the tray on his lap before he spun around to go out the back toward the court Robin had put in shortly after he'd bought the estate.

Robin had had the path paved once Quinn's three month trial period had been up and everyone had agreed he'd stay on for the rest of the contract. He appreciated the care that Robin had shown, remodeling things around the estate and the house to accommodate Quinn's handicaps. He'd paved quite a few paths around the grounds and had got a chair installed to help Quinn get in and out of the pool easier.

After the Australian Open, Robin had had Quinn's patio redone to include a gorgeous foundation and a beautiful meditation area for him. It actually reminded him a lot of his spot back at his house in Colorado. A thought hit him and he wondered if Robin hadn't talked to Morgan about it.

As he approached the court, he heard the sound of a racquet hitting a ball, the squeak of shoes on the hard surface, and a loud grunt as someone returned the ball. He couldn't see which one it was. Jerome had come over to hit with Robin earlier and they'd been out there for two hours so far.

Margerite had made enough for all of them to snack on, so he'd hang out with them a little bit before the car got there. When he got to the gate, he saw Robin toss the ball high in the air then serve, dropping the ball in the ad court for Jerome to hit back. He didn't say anything until Robin missed a return.

"Hey, you two, I brought some snacks," he called.

"Awesome. You're giving me a chance to rest from getting my ass kicked by this bastard," Jerome said as he jogged over to open the gate for him.

He allowed Jerome to take the tray off his lap so he could get his chair over the slight bump of the threshold. It was funny that Jerome had been the one who never asked him whether he needed help or not. He just did things to ease Quinn's way without it being him sucking up. So while Quinn did think Jerome was an annoying jackass at times, he did find that he liked the guy, even after it had come out that Jerome's maid was the one who spilled Robin's secrets.

"Thanks."

Robin stalked over to the table before throwing himself down into the chair. Quinn winced at the obvious sign that he was still mad at him. They'd already had it out the night before when Quinn had announced he was leaving. His contract had nearly another month to go on it, but he didn't see the point of hanging around any longer.

It was time for Robin to sink or swim on his own. Quinn had given him all the tools to keep his body and mind in peak condition. As much as he wanted to stay, Robin hadn't given him a reason to. All he'd said was Quinn's contract was for a year and the year wasn't up. Quinn had checked with Ramsey and Stein, both of whom had said they were fine with Quinn leaving early if he wanted.

What he really wanted was for Robin to tell him he loved him, but he was pretty sure that wasn't going to happen, especially since Robin hadn't said anything last night when they'd talked. Could that be because Robin had been waiting for Quinn to leave before hooking back up with Danie? Well, if that was the truth then he should be happy that Robin hadn't slept with the Afrikaner while they were together.

"You call for a car?" Robin asked while reaching for a strawberry.

"Yes. Margerite says it'll be here soon." Quinn glanced over at Jerome. "You keep doing well playing doubles, Jerome, you'll win a lot more Major tournaments. Especially if you focus more on your play and less on how attractive your mixed doubles partner is."

"Yeah. Yeah." Jerome flopped his hand in a dismissive motion. "It's not like I don't hear that from Coach all the time."

Quinn chuckled.

"Are you heading home now?" Robin fidgeted with his water bottle and didn't look at him.

"Actually no. Morgan's meeting me in Bern then we were going to wander around Switzerland and the rest of Europe. Somehow he got the leave and suggested we do some hiking. Before the accident, I wanted to do some mountain climbing in the Alps." He patted his thigh. "Well, climbing might be beyond me now, but checking out some different countries isn't."

"Sounds like fun," Robin muttered.

He wanted to reach out and take Robin's hand, but he wasn't sure Robin would welcome that. "Maybe we could show up in Paris for the Open. See you win."

"Give me a call if you do and I'll make sure there are some passes left for you." Robin shot him a glance that somehow looked bitter and hopeful at the same time. "You'll stay in touch, right? Come watch me play in some other tournaments if you have time."

"Of course." He took Robin's hand in his, squeezing it tight. "I'm not abandoning you, Robin. I'm just going to hang out with my brother. If you want, I'll make sure we're in Paris for the Open."

Robin was about to say something, but Margerite appeared and announced that the car was there.

Jerome jumped to his feet. "I've gotta take a piss. I'll be back in a few."

They watched him race away toward the house then Quinn met Robin's gaze for a minute before he leaned over to kiss him. Robin clutched his shoulders as he opened to let Quinn sweep his tongue in. He sighed when Robin slipped his hands into his hair, giving it a little tug. He let the kiss go on for a few seconds longer before he started to pull away.

"I have to go. The car's waiting," he murmured.

"I know. Take care and tell Morgan hey for me." Robin pushed to his feet. "Do you want me to walk you out?"

"Nah. You can stay here." He didn't think he'd be able to leave if he turned around to watch Robin disappear from the back of the car window. "I'll call you when I get to Bern and the hotel where I'm meeting Morgan."

"Okay." Robin bent to brush a quick kiss over his lips. "Thanks for everything, Quinn. You helped me save my ass and my career."

"I'm not going to say it's my job, even though it is. This time it was more than that. I care for you, Robin, and want to see you succeed." Quinn cradled Robin's face. "You need to know you can do it all on your own, though you won't technically be alone. You have Ramsey, Stein and Margerite to help you. Plus I'm sure Danie will be around to listen to you as well. We'll plan on meeting in Paris."

Robin nodded then Quinn whirled his chair around, heading back toward the house. He wanted to leave as fast as possible, now that he'd said goodbye.

Margerite had already taken his duffle and suitcase to the driver. She'd also made sure his prosthetics were in the backseat of the car so he could put them on when they gotten close to Bern. After getting himself situated in the backseat, Quinn motioned for the driver to take his wheelchair.

Once all of that was done, the door was shut and the car began to move down the driveway. Quinn leaned his head against the seat, closing his eyes for a moment. His heart hurt. Falling in love with Robin had been so easy that Quinn had never really realized when it had happened, but he still couldn't bring himself to tell the man.

Sighing, he tried to lift his spirits with the thought that he would see Robin in a few weeks in Paris. Even if Morgan didn't want to go, Quinn planned on showing up because he just knew Robin would win the Open and wipe away the horrible loss he'd suffered the year before.

As they turned out of the drive, Quinn was able to see the solitary figure standing by the house for a brief moment, then he was gone.

Chapter Twenty-Two

"Coach will meet you outside Court Two with your credentials, so you and Morgan can come and go without getting in trouble or stopped all the time," Robin informed Quinn over the phone. "You have his number to text in case you miss one another."

"Awesome. I know I won't be able to see you before your match, but can we get together afterward?" He really wanted to talk to Robin in person.

After spending the last couple of weeks wandering and hiking around Switzerland and Europe, he'd discovered just how much he missed Robin. He'd confessed his feelings to Morgan, and his brother had recommended he just lay everything on the line with Robin and see where that went.

"Of course. I'd really like to see you. I'll send you the address of the place I'm renting for the tournament. You can go there after the match, unless you want to hang out and watch some other ones." Robin sounded a little distracted.

"That would be great. I'm not a big tennis fan, so watching anyone else besides you doesn't mean much to me." Quinn had told Robin that before. "Good luck and I'll see you after the match."

"Thanks. Coach will be out there in about ten minutes." Robin hung up.

Quinn stuck his phone in his pocket then glanced around to see where Morgan was standing. When his brother saw him, he walked over.

"We getting in?" Morgan asked once he came stand next to him.

He nodded. "Yeah. Ramsey will be here in a few minutes to give us our credentials that will get us into the player's box and stuff without having to worry about being checked all the time."

Morgan snorted. "I could've gotten us those."

"Whatever. After the match, I'm going to head over to Robin's and we're going to talk. I'm taking your advice."

He grinned as Morgan clapped him on the shoulder.

"Good for you, Ace. You need to get things sorted out. You know I'm behind you no matter what, but I'm thinking you won't be moving back to Colorado to live anyway." Morgan grinned.

"Quinn. Morgan."

They turned to see Ramsey strolling toward them. He seemed happy to see him and that eased Quinn a little. He knew he wasn't going to give Robin up, even if Ramsey didn't like him, but it would certainly help.

"Here. Robin's in the locker room getting ready for his first match." Ramsey handed him and Morgan lanyards with badges hooked on them. "These will get you pretty much anywhere you want to go. I'm glad you're back, Quinn."

"How's he been since I left?" He'd called and texted Robin a few times, but they hadn't really talked about Robin's playing. He put the lanyard around his neck.

Ramsey shrugged. "He's not been happy, but amazingly he's not let it affect his playing. He remains focused and determined while he's training and playing. It's when he gets home that he kind of closed off from the rest of us."

"He's not drinking again, is he?" That was one of the things Quinn had worried about. While he was pretty sure Robin had figured out how stupid it was to drink while playing, sometimes when upset, it was easier to fall back into bad habits.

"No. He's not. Robin actually meditates like you showed him to do and all that." Ramsey gestured toward the entrance. "Let's go sit and we can chat. Jerome is already there."

"Stein not here?" Quinn headed toward the gates.

Ramsey pointed in the direction Quinn needed to go in to get to the player's boxes. "No. Alfred doesn't usually show up until the later rounds. It's just his superstition. Good thing Robin's been going further and further in the tournaments."

"I've been listening to the pundits. They're thinking he might have a really good shot at winning this year, which is amazing consider how early he lost last year." Morgan paused at the bottom of the stairs along with Quinn.

Taking a deep breath, Quinn grabbed a hold of the railing and started to climb. There weren't many steps, but he'd been on his feet most of the day and his knees were beginning to ache. He winced when he stubbed his foot against one of the stairs and it jolted through his leg.

"Just a little bit further then take a right. Go down to the box on the left at the bottom of the stairs on the court," Ramsey told him.

As he got there, Jerome glanced up from his phone. "Hey there, Quinn. Great to see you, man."

He shook Jerome's hand then sat, sighing as he stretched. "When's your first match?"

"I'm doing doubles, so tomorrow." Jerome grimaced then smiled. "It's great to know that you care enough to come watch Robin play."

"Of course I care about him." Quinn didn't want to discuss it with Jerome before Robin. "What are his chances against this guy?"

Jerome pursed his lips while he thought. "They're actually pretty good. Robin's playing like a mad man. You were the best thing to come along in his life this past year. You got him out of his head and focused back on tennis and winning. He's back to the old Robin before the drinking and stuff."

"That's good." Quinn leaned back in his seat and smiled as he heard the announcer introduce Robin, then watched him walk out on court, followed by a similar entrance for his opponent.

* * * *

Robin dried off after his post-match shower then began to put on his street clothes. It was hard to tell whether the utter relief Robin felt was because he'd gotten through his first round at Roland Garros, or because Quinn had actually shown up. He'd said he would, but then again, people changed their minds about things, especially when they were apart.

He hadn't had time to sit and mope about how crushed he'd been when Quinn had left. Something had clicked over inside him when he'd seen Quinn's car disappear from sight that day—a sort of determination that he wouldn't take this as the final word. He was going to get Quinn back.

Robin had nearly jumped in the car to follow him then realized he had no idea where in Bern Quinn was even going to meet Morgan. And that would have been pathetic. No—he was going to take a different route. Quinn seemed to think that Robin needed time to make it on his own, so he was going to pour every bit of himself into proving to Quinn that he *could* live without him...but didn't want to.

He'd hit the last couple of tournaments between then and the French with a renewed sense of purpose, and his top four results in each had been gratifying, but not enough. Every time he'd caught himself reaching for the phone to call Quinn, he'd stopped and reminded himself that he shouldn't be selfish— after all, Quinn was right in the middle of something he'd always wanted to do with his brother. It would be pretty selfish to take away from that family time.

That had made him think of his own family, and he'd decided to pay his aunt and uncle a surprise visit. They'd been shocked to see him, but he'd refused to leave without speaking to them. After some heated words and a lot of tears, he'd finally convinced his aunt—Mom—that he wasn't going to fall down the same pit as her sister had, that he was making strides to changes his habits and live a more purposeful, aware lifestyle. Once she'd been convinced, her husband had followed suit, only having gone along with her drastic reaction out of caring for her, because of how much fear and pain the reports on Robin had brought up for her.

Then he'd told them he was gay.

It had been rather anticlimactic. He'd braced himself for an about-face on their reconciliation owing to their very strict religious beliefs. However, perhaps because of how far they'd come and the estrangement they'd suffered, they'd taken the news rather well, all things considered. The whole thing had been a huge relief, a weight lifted that he hadn't even realized had been putting a huge strain on him.

He'd offered to fly them in for part of the French, but because it was so last minute — and probably because the elderly couple had had enough upheaval in their orderly lives just then — they admitted they'd prefer to travel to Wimbledon instead of Paris. So when he'd left, it was with a much lighter heart and the promise of seeing them in England in less than two months. He'd hoped in a small, secret part of his heart that they'd get to meet Quinn there and they'd all get along and...

Yeah, turned out Robin was a bit of a romantic. But he still wished for that very same thing. And today he was one step closer, because Quinn was actually here in Paris.

Waiting to see him while Robin lollygagged in the changing room.

Robin sighed, butterflies churning his stomach. Yes, he was procrastinating a little bit. He wondered if they had left the grounds yet. He almost texted and told Quinn and Morgan to wait for him rather than meet him at his Paris rental. He'd secured an apartment this year instead of returning to the small hotel he usually stayed at. He hadn't wanted anything associated with the bad memories of the previous year, which had meant a change of living space. And if he was being truthful, he'd have to admit that he'd chosen it with Quinn in mind. He was more than likely planning to stay with Morgan somewhere, but in case he wanted to...

"Don't get ahead of yourself, Robin."

He finally got himself sorted out then packed up his bags to head out. He wasn't terribly surprised to see Jerome waiting for him as he emerged, though he would have expected Coach Ramsey to be with him. Waving off the usher who began to accompany him, he greeted his friend.

"Congratulations on your big win, stud." Jerome gave him a backslapping hug then took one of his bags and shouldered it.

Robin raised an eyebrow at him as they started to walk together. "Thanks, but it wasn't *that* big."

"Oh, right. And congratulations on the match, too, but I was talking about Quinn showing up."

Oh. Robin flushed and smacked his so-called buddy. "Where's Coach?"

"He's helping Morgan and Quinn get to a car. Quinn's pretty tired..." Jerome waved a hand vaguely toward his legs.

Robin could only imagine how much his legs must be aching if he was wearing his prosthetics like he always did at matches. Most of the player's boxes weren't accessible, so he made do.

"Wait, are they still here?" He quickened his pace.

"Probably. It took a while to get out of the stands through the masses of your fans. I've never heard such one-sided cheering for someone who's not French here before."

It had been truly gratifying...when he'd heard it. He tended to tune out the crowd during matches—had to. But especially on long points, he'd gotten rousing reactions from the crowd.

There. Robin's breath caught at the sight of Quinn just about to get into the back of a hired car, with

Morgan and Coach nearby. When Morgan closed the door rather than get in with Quinn, Robin panicked.

"Hey! Morgan!"

Morgan spun to take him in then quickly prevented the driver from pulling away. Robin finally reached them, barely noticing when Morgan took his remaining bag to hand to the driver, so focused was he on the opening door.

"See you later," someone said as he climbed in then the door closed behind him with a thump.

He gazed at Quinn for the first time in weeks, taking everything in. His new haircut, the glow of a recent sunburn, a shirt he hadn't seen before.

"Hey there." Quinn's voice was low and intimate as the car pulled away.

"Hi." Conscious of the driver, he restrained himself from climbing onto Quinn's lap and settled for taking his hand.

Quinn gripped it back tightly, almost painful for a moment, before he eased up. "Good match."

"I'm glad you could come."

The banal conversation was a paper-thin cover for the messages that their body language and eyes were exchanging. Like magnets finally close enough to react, they came together solidly and unwilling to separate. Thank God the apartment was close by, though traffic was heavy.

They finally arrived having barely spoken a dozen words. Robin collected his bag, while Quinn took his time getting out and moving where Robin indicated to enter the building. The doorman greeted them with a surprise—Quinn's wheelchair and one of his suitcases.

"How the—?" Quinn started to say, then they exchanged a look and said together, "Morgan."

The ancient elevator got them to their floor—well, within a few inches anyway—and shortly they were closed away from the world.

"Let me show you my room," Robin finally broke the silence.

"Robin, I'm sorry."

"Come on, you need to get off your legs." Robin walked away, pushing Quinn's chair with his bag on it, knowing that Quinn would follow.

"Robin—"

He didn't stop until they'd reached his bedroom door. "I'm not sorry. You did the right thing."

"It was a crappy way to handle it."

Robin shrugged. "Maybe, but it was effective. Let's not talk about anything deep yet. Maybe after the Open, okay?" Because if this was temporary, if Quinn wasn't coming back to him, he didn't want to know it and have to go out and try to play without his heart. "I just want to enjoy being with you for however long we have together."

"I want—"

He pressed his fingers to Quinn's lips. "Soon. Legs off." He turned away and busied himself turning down the sheets before beginning to strip out of his clothes.

Quinn finally got with the program and sat on the edge of the bed to begin the process. Robin lay with his head propped on his hand and watched until Quinn was as naked as he was. He had a momentary flicker of doubt when Quinn turned over and he wasn't very hard, but the gentle way Quinn gathered him into his arms soon assuaged his worry.

"I missed you," he whispered against Robin's lips before stealing his breath with a soul-deep kiss.

Robin couldn't speak but he showed him with his touch, relearning Quinn's body and seeking out his hot spots. Their explorations soon turned carnal as they reacted to the reunion, wanting to please each other. Not wanting to let go long enough to prep for anything more, Robin brought Quinn's hand between them and clasped both of their cocks between their combined grips. After weeks apart, stroking and thrusting together while tangling their tongues, their breathing increasingly rough, they didn't take long to come, one after the other.

Robin fought back his emotions as he clung to Quinn in the aftermath of the very hot frottage. He knew they still had a big conversation coming at some point, but for right now, he was exactly where he wanted to be — back in Quinn's arms.

Chapter Twenty-Three

When the door opened, Quinn looked up from where he sat in the living room. He'd gone on ahead back to the apartment rental after watching the awards presentation ceremony immediately following the French Open's final match. He knew there were going to be a ton of interviews Robin had to do before he'd be able to come home. Quinn had reached the limit of wearing his legs, so at the first opportunity he'd given Robin a discreet kiss on the back of the neck, whispering that he would meet Robin back at their place.

Robin grinned at him and he couldn't do anything except hold open his arms. He grunted when Robin slammed into him, causing him to fall back onto the couch. Quinn wrapped one of his arms around Robin's waist, the other around his shoulder to cup the back of his head. He crushed their lips together and Robin melted into his embrace.

Soon they were rocking against each other, and the sounds Robin was making turned Quinn on to the point where he wanted to strip him naked and fuck him right there. Unfortunately, they didn't have any supplies, so he eased Robin away.

"No," Robin whined.

Quinn chuckled. "Don't worry. I just think we need to move this to the bed. Our supplies are in there. I didn't think about bringing any out to the living room with me."

"Okay." Robin jumped up then held out his hand to help him sit up. "I'll head to the bedroom and get naked."

He didn't wait for Quinn's reply before he took off. Quinn got himself into his chair then rolled down the hallway to where Robin waited for him. When he got there, he inhaled sharply at the sight of Robin sprawled on the mattress. The sheets and blankets had been stripped down to the foot of the bed. The bottle of lube and a couple of foil packets were on the pillow next to Robin's head.

He moved to the side where he could reach out and trail his fingers over Robin's leg up to where his thigh connected to his hip. Robin shuddered as Quinn leaned over to suck up a mark on his hip.

"You need to be in here with me," Robin told him.

"Yes, sir." Quinn tugged his T-shirt off, tossing it across the room, not caring where it landed. He poked Robin's side. "You need to slide over."

After Robin made room, Quinn swung from the chair to the bed. He wiggled out of his sweats, setting them on the seat of his wheelchair. He lay on his side then wrapped his arm around Robin to pull him close, his chest to Robin's back. Brushing a kiss over the nape of Robin's neck, he ran his hand down over Robin's chest to his groin.

He rubbed his cock along Robin's crease. "Put some lube on my fingers," he ordered and Robin did as he was told.

Once they were coated, he brought them back to caress Robin's hole. Robin pushed back slightly, silently begging for him to do more. Quinn knew exactly what Robin wanted, so he pressed just the tip of his middle finger against Robin's opening.

"Don't tease me," Robin pleaded.

"I wouldn't do that to you, love," he whispered against Robin's skin as he pushed both of his fingers in. He wasn't interested in extending the foreplay. Quinn wanted to fuck Robin as fast and hard as he could.

He stretched Robin quickly then arranged them so that he could thrust into Robin while they were on their sides. They moved together in that carnal rhythm they'd developed early on during sex. It was obvious how well they fit together.

"God, Robin, you're so fucking tight," Quinn managed to say as he stroked his cock in and out of Robin's ass while pumping his hand up and down Robin's length.

Robin didn't seem able to say anything, just seemed overwhelmed by emotions. He trembled in Quinn's arms, rocking between Quinn's erection and his hand.

"Robin, I'm going to come," Quinn warned before his climax hit him, sending cum to flood the condom. He continued to move until he heard Robin cry out and moist heat covered his hand.

He held Robin while he calmed his breathing and kissed Robin's shoulder. They both shuddered when Quinn's softened cock started to slide from Robin. He reached down to grab it, making sure the condom didn't come off. After rolling on to his back, he snagged some tissues and took care of the rubber, tossing it in the wastebasket next to the bed.

There was a damp cloth and a towel on the nightstand, so he wiped himself and Robin off then tossed both cloths in the direction of the bathroom. Robin hadn't really moved during the whole experience. Finally when Quinn had settled back down, Robin rolled over so they were lying face-to-face.

"Did you call me love?"

Quinn cringed inside, but he knew it was time to admit how he felt. He'd spent the time away from Robin wishing the man was with him. Morgan had gotten sick of him talking about Robin all the time. Eventually Morgan had told him to man up and confess he loved Robin. Then when they'd got to Paris for the Open, Morgan had told Quinn that he better not come back to Colorado to live. That Morgan expected to be getting a phone call telling him to pack up all of Quinn's things and ship them to Switzerland.

He placed his hand on Robin's cheek and nodded. "I did. I love you, Robin, and it took being away from you these last few weeks to finally get myself to admit that. I want to come live with you—not just as your personal chef—but as your boyfriend and partner."

Robin's eyes widened and Quinn saw surprise and caring in them, but was there love mingled in there as well? Could he be so lucky?

Robin's heart was beating so fast he wondered whether it was audible to Quinn. The stupid thing hadn't learned its lesson, obviously, even though Robin's brain had scolded it for a month for being so gullible. Right now, his heart was apparently doing a victory dance, one that had started the moment Robin had heard the L-word. It made him a little giddy.

"Okay, not to get demanding right off the bat, but are you okay with having just one extremely long-term client for the rest of your life? Because I really don't want you to go live with anyone else to do your job. I missed you too much...but don't worry, I can make it without you. I just don't want to have to, if you know what I mean..."

When Robin finally ran out of breath he grimaced. Maybe that wasn't the best reaction to being told Quinn loved him, based on Quinn's astonished expression, but in his defense it was the first thing that came to mind and something he'd been thinking about ever since Quinn had left.

The import of what Quinn had just said hit him at last. Oh God, how weird was he. He hung his head for a moment then cleared his throat and looked at Quinn. "I meant to say, I love you too."

"I think the 'rest of your life' part was a good indication of that, but it's nice to hear the actual words." Thankfully Quinn was smiling. "I always knew you could make it on your own, but I needed to make sure you knew it as well. And about the job— that's a good point I don't want you to have to worry about for a minute longer. I don't have to be a live-in to do what I do—and don't plan to with anyone else. But I can still offer consultations and develop menu plans for clients. It'll work out," he promised.

Robin relaxed. It was good to hear that Quinn wasn't going to have to give up a job that meant so much to him.

The rest of what had kept him so busy over that past few weeks popped into his head and he grinned. "I can't wait to get you home."

Epilogue

Quinn practically groaned in relief when the car pulled up to Robin's house. After the flight from Paris to Bern, they'd taken a car to Lucerne, and Quinn was ready to get his prosthetics off and relax for the rest of the day. They'd stayed in Paris for a couple of days after the tournament, just wandering around to see the sights. Morgan had gone off on his own, not upset at all that his little brother had dumped him.

Of course, since Morgan knew Quinn and Robin were in love, he had said they needed to spend some time alone in the city of love. Quinn had rolled his eyes when Morgan had told him that, but he had to admit it had been romantic to have dinner in view of the Eiffel Tower all lit up at night.

The driver opened the back door for them and he slid out, finding his balance on the driveway before moving to the side, letting Robin out. He glanced up at the front of the 'castle' Robin owned. His eyes widened when he saw that the stairs had been replaced with a stone ramp.

"What did you do?" He looked over at Robin who grinned at him.

"It'll make your life easier, won't it?" Robin gestured toward the ramp. "Alfred said something to me about how he hid the first ramp to the side so it didn't ruin the facade of the house. I don't care about that."

Without thinking, Quinn leaned forward to press a kiss to Robin's mouth. "Thank you, though you didn't have to do that. I didn't mind. I got the whole not wanting to destroy the look of the building."

"Let's go in."

The driver had carried their bags inside for them while they talked, so when they got inside, Quinn saw them sitting near the stairs.

"I guess I didn't think about the room situation," he muttered as he stared at the flight of stairs leading up to the second floor.

"I wasn't sure what you would like. I thought about having an elevator put in, but I couldn't figure out where to put it. Then I thought about one of those lift chairs." Robin shrugged.

Quinn chuckled. "You don't have to worry about that. There's a set of stairs in the back, going up from the kitchen, so we can put the chair there. I know you don't care about the look of your place, but I'd rather it wasn't out where people could see it."

Robin nodded. "That's fine with me. Whatever we have to do to make living here comfortable for you."

He let Robin take his hand and pull him down the hallway into the kitchen. As soon as they stepped into the room, Quinn felt his mouth drop open. The entire kitchen had been renovated to accommodate Quinn. The island counter had two different levels now. One he could reach while in his wheelchair and one normal height for him when he used his prosthetics. It was like that all around the area and Quinn turned to look at Robin.

"When did you do this?"

Robin dropped his gaze for a second then met his. "The day after you left. I paid like, twice the cost, to get it done asap since I knew I'd be seeing you in Paris and I wanted to ask you to come back here so we could talk about things."

"Well good thing we got our talking done with, huh?" Quinn wandered around, running his hands over the new counters and the refrigerator. "This is beyond amazing, Robin. I never expected this."

"I wanted to show you that I was committed to this relationship." Waving his hand in a vague gesture, Robin included not just the kitchen but the ramp and probably a ton of other renovations he'd done for Quinn that he hadn't seen yet. "I know it was your job, but you did so much for me to get me back on track, along with giving me a man I could fall in love with. I just wanted to do something for you."

"In case you convinced me to move in with you," Quinn said as he bumped Robin's hip with his.

"Yeah, though I was willing to compromise and see if you'd come visit me as many times as you could throughout the year. We could also meet up at different tournaments."

Quinn touched Robin's lips with his finger, stopping him from babbling. "We already talked about this, love. I'm going to move here, but keep my place in Colorado. It'll give us a chance to get away somewhere without any tennis involved. That way you can get a break from it once in a while. Plus I want to make sure Morgan has some place to hide when he needs to."

Robin wrapped his arms around Quinn's waist and Quinn let him pull him close. He nuzzled Robin's jaw then dropped a kiss on his cheek.

"Thank you for everything you've done to make your house a home for me," he whispered.

"You've become my home, Quinn, no matter where we are in the world. Are you ready to travel the world with me?" Robin leaned back to look at him.

"I can't think of anyone else I'd rather follow around," Quinn admitted then kissed Robin. "Agreeing to work for you was the best decision I ever made."

About the Authors

T.A. Chase

There is beauty in every kind of love, so why not live a life without boundaries? Experiencing everything the world offers fascinates TA and writing about the things that make each of us unique is how she shares those insights. When not writing, TA's watching movies, reading and living life to the fullest.

Devon Rhodes

Devon started reading and writing at an early age and never looked back. At 39 and holding, Devon finally figured out the best way to channel her midlife crisis was to morph from mild-mannered stay-at-home mom to erotic romance writer. She lives in Oregon with her family, who are (mostly) understanding of all the time she spends on her laptop, aka the black hole.

T.A. Chase and Devon Rhodes love to hear from readers. You can find their contact information, website details and author profile pages at http://www.totallybound.com.

Totally Bound Publishing